PRINT EDITION

Legend of the Timekeepers © 2015 by Mirror World Publishing and Sharon Ledwith

Edited by: Justine Dowsett

Published by Mirror World Publishing in August, 2015

All Rights Reserved.

   *This book is a work of fiction. All of the characters, organizations and events portrayed in this novel are either products of the authors' imagination or are used fictitiously. Any resemblance to actual locales, events or persons is entirely coincidental.

Mirror World Publishing

Windsor, Ontario

www.mirrorworldpublishing.com

info@mirrorworldpublishing.com

ISBN: 978-1-987976-05-2

For my mother, Peggy.

You taught me to stand up for myself, and never forget my roots.

Legend of the Timekeepers

Sharon Ledwith

M|W mirror world publishing

Prologue

"*I* have decided. We are leaving Atlantis by the end of the week."

Lilith raised her head from the scroll she'd been studying. Had she heard her father correctly? *We're leaving Atlantis?*

A tremor shook the small marble table where she was sitting. Two embroidered chairs near the open porch vibrated across the white floor until they smacked into a column decorated with gold and silver butterflies. The wide chairs fell back with a clatter. Lilith braced herself, knowing that her unstable country was falling apart bit by bit. She ducked under the table just as a bronze tile fell from the ceiling and missed her head.

Her father gasped. "Lilith! Are you all right?"

Dizzy, she patted her head, making sure her ivory hairpins still held her long, fair hair in place. "Yes, Father, I'm fine."

"Segund, I told you to leave a week ago!" her uncle shouted as he entered the room. "If I had a child as young as Lilith, I would have had her on the first boat out of Atlantis!"

Lilith got up so fast her vision blurred. She shook her head vigorously. "I am not a young child, Uncle Kukulkan!" She stomped her foot for effect, almost knocking off her palm-leaf sandal. "I'll be ten soon!"

Kukulkan grinned at her. His long, full red beard bristled and he soothed it with a large, tanned hand. Then his face turned serious.

Legend of the Timekeepers

He walked toward Lilith, his shadow engulfing her smaller frame, and crouched to meet her eye to eye. Matching sea-blue eyes stared at each other before her uncle raised his hand to adjust a dislodged hairpin. He sighed deeply, then with his long thumb, he grazed her high cheekbone and let it run down the length of her face to tweak her firm chin.

"Your mother, Meg would be proud of you, Lilith. My wife would have been as well. Unfortunately, they were taken away from us far too soon."

Tears welled in Lilith's eyes. She'd lost both her mother and her Aunt Ambeno about a year ago while they were inside one of the amphitheatres in the City of the Golden Gates during a terrible earthquake. A huge marble statue of Belial fell and instantly crushed the group of people standing under it. Her mother and aunt had been among them.

"Leave the past in the past, Kukulkan." Segund waved a hand. "It is what it is."

Kukulkan stood and turned toward Segund. The two brothers were almost identical in stature and looks, except her father's hair was the color of the sun and his beard wasn't as full and long. Lilith allowed herself a deep breath. *Father looks so tired.* His broad shoulders sagged more and more lately, and his crinkled white linen shirt and dark blue pants looked like they hadn't been washed in days. He twisted the thick, gold ring in the shape of a snake on his middle left finger long enough to notice Lilith staring at him and stopped.

Kukulkan patted her father's shoulder. "I'm sorry, Segund, I know you have an important job trying to organize the evacuation of Atlantis. Your eyes and face tell me you are weary. Did you manage to get all of the arches to safety?"

"Only the seventh arch, so far. The rest are prepared and ready, awaiting shipment to the other destinations I have chosen. I have decided that Lilith and I will be going where I sent the seventh arch."

Lilith narrowed her fair brows. "Where's the seventh arch gone, Father?"

He smiled, revealing his pearl-white teeth. "To the Black Land."

Did I hear Father correctly? The Black Land? Lilith balled her fists and slammed them against the sides of her slim hips. "But...but, Father, there are snakes in the Black Land! Poisonous

8

snakes with hoods that make their scaly, ugly heads bigger! I am not going there! I want to go with Uncle Kukulkan!"

Kukulkan stifled a chuckle. Segund gave his older brother an angry stare and turned his attention back to Lilith. "Now, Lilith, you've simply got to get over this fear of snakes you have. After all, we are known to the world as the Serpent People."

Lilith pursed her lips. "That's because of the human-snake hybrids the dark magi created!"

"That is not the reason, Lilith," Segund said, tapping the tip of her nose. "Serpents know the earth better than any other creature and Atlanteans understand this. Serpents teach us how to transmute the poison of our experiences into healing energy to share with the rest of the world."

"Your father is correct," Kukulkan said. "Besides, there are snakes living in the western land where I'm going too. Long, thick snakes that wrap around your body and slowly squeeze you to death before they eat you."

Lilith squealed and covered her mouth.

Segund slapped his brother across the back of his head. "You're not helping, feather-brain!"

Kukulkan rubbed his head. He winked at Lilith. "Don't worry, Lilith, your father will keep you safe from these poisonous, hooded snakes."

Another tremor shook the white marble tiles beneath their feet, and a crack that resembled a long serpent crept up between Lilith and her remaining family members, cutting them off from each other. Crystal dishes on granite shelves next to the large, stone fireplace in the main room crashed to the floor. Lilith jumped and hugged herself, feeling her soft linen top cling to her sweaty body like an oyster stuck in its shell.

Segund leaped over the crack and snatched his daughter up in his strong arms. He hugged her fiercely. "No harm will come to you, Lilith. I'll see to that. I promise on your mother's honor."

Lilith pushed her face under her father's warm neck, smelling the stale sweat of these last few days and feeling his rapid pulse against her cheek. His soft beard gave her small comfort. Her hands crept around his neck, and she reached for the clump of crystals that held his long hair in place. This calmed her instantly, took away the unknowingness. She pushed back and stared into his eyes.

Legend of the Timekeepers

"That's a silly thing to promise, Father. If Mother was here, she would say that all we have is now."

"When did you start getting so wise, Lilith?" Kukulkan asked, jumping the narrow fissure

Segund smiled. "I believe she takes after Meg in that department, Kukulkan."

He laughed. "And her Aunt Ambeno!"

Screams pierced the air like tiny daggers, making Lilith shudder. The doomsday prophecy was really happening. Maybe not tonight, but soon Atlantis would crumble and sink into the ocean. This horrific event had been predicted over one hundred years ago by the House of Seers, after the first major earthquake destroyed the southwestern portion of Atlantis. A year in advance of the time of destruction, Lilith's father planned the mass exodus with the king's permission. Many Atlanteans had left immediately, some going west to where Uncle Kukulkan was heading, others toward the north where it was colder, and the rest sailing east to the dry climate of the Black Land. Then there were those who had decided to stay, debunking the seers, calling their bluff, saying Atlantis would never die.

"You can put me down now, Father. We need to start packing before this place falls apart."

Kukulkan's brows rose. "How is it that you're not afraid of the earth trembling and crumbling around us, but you freeze at the mere mention of a sna—"

"You know it's your fault, Uncle!" Lilith snapped and wagged a finger.

Segund sighed, then gently put her down. "I'm afraid Lilith's got you there, Kukulkan."

"How was I to know Lilith would react the way she did when I showed her what I bought for her from a merchant trader? I thought it would make a great pet!" Kukulkan shrugged. "Poseidon knows, she needs to get her nose out of those scrolls she studies and get outside more often. I thought the snake would help her connect better with nature."

"Well, it didn't!" Lilith felt her chest harden, her fingers curled into a fist. "You woke me from my nap and put that snake in my bed! You scared me! I felt so trapped, so helpless! It could have eaten me!"

10

Kukulkan grunted. "I would not give you anything that could harm you, Lilith, understand that."

Lilith realized she had been holding her body tight. She took a breath and let it out like her mother had taught her to do when she was upset. "I believe you, Uncle, I do, it's just that...that when I opened my eyes and saw the snake staring at me, its dark eyes never blinking, and its long forked tongue flicking out to taste my cheek..." She retched, tasting a sour gob in her mouth.

"I see. Then, I trust you have no use for this?" He reached into his jewel-encrusted satchel attached to his embroidered sash roped around his soft purple robe. "It belonged to your aunt. She wanted you to have this when you became of age, but fate has not been on our side." Kukulkan passed the shiny object to Lilith.

She stared at it. At first, she made a face. It was a coiled snake bracelet. Immediately, she knew it was made of orichalcum. The brilliant hue of pink made it appear shinier than gold. Individual scales were etched to perfection going in an upward pattern until reaching the snake's head. Tiny diamonds were embedded into the mouth for teeth, and two sapphires—the size of her fingernails—were used for the eyes. It was a masterpiece created by a master artisan. Although the bracelet looked heavy, Lilith knew better. The pair of orichalcum dolphin statues on her father's desk was double its size, and each weighed no more than a pomegranate. Lilith reached out to touch it just as another tremor exploded, rippling through her body.

Kukulkan grabbed her before she fell. "We need to leave. Now!"

Segund stumbled and reached for the closest pillar. "But...I need to get the five other arches on their appropriate ships with the keepers I have chosen and trained. They must leave when I leave. The arches are our only direct contact with the Children of the Law of One and will make sure our race is preserved, and that this old, red land doesn't disappear forever."

Lilith's insides jiggled like a beached jellyfish during a storm. She clasped her hands. Her father had been named the Keeper of the Arches years before she was born. His purpose was to receive the messages sent through the arches from the Children of the Law of One, and then share them with the appropriate Atlanteans in authority. Lilith knew these ethereal messengers were wise and kind, and they taught that everyone and everything living on the Earth was interrelated and interdependent. To disrespect another

Legend of the Timekeepers

person was to disrespect yourself. It was a simple way, and many Atlanteans followed this doctrine. But there were those who opposed the Law of One, those who were immoral and corrupt. Lilith's stomach clenched at the thought.

"It will do no good if the Keeper of the Arches succumbs with Atlantis" Kukulkan replied, shaking his head. "At least the seventh arch is safe. And you know as well as I do that the fifth arch has been gone from here for over one hundred years."

Lilith's father snorted, making his nostrils flare in an undignified manner. "The fifth arch might as well be destroyed, seeing as it is in Belial's possession. That evil magus has been draining the arch's spiral energy long enough by using it to control the people in the country he landed in. And if they don't submit to him, he sacrifices or enslaves them. I thank Poseidon that you've been chosen by the Children of the Law of One to go deal with Belial personally."

Kukulkan's jaw tensed. "And I shall not disappoint, my brother. The survival of our culture, our race, and this old red land's memory depends on it."

An eruption from Mount Atlas shook all of them. More screams resounded outside their stately home, with its flowering vines winding around the balcony, that overlooked the ocean. Lilith wrung her hands. She had gotten used to the instability of her country, the frequent quakes and mini-eruptions. She knew they must go. They had no choice if they wanted to live. In truth, their house hadn't been a home since her mother had been taken from them. Lilith felt a slight tug on her arm and unclasped her hands. She hadn't realized she'd been staring into space until she looked down at her left arm. Uncle Kukulkan had wound her aunt's snake bracelet around her forearm. It was loose and awkward. The bracelet wouldn't stay up and slid down to imprison her hand.

Lilith wrinkled her nose. "It doesn't fit."

He laughed. "Don't worry you'll grow into it, Lilith."

"It's still a snake," she said, grimacing. "I don't think I'll ever learn to like it."

He lightly touched her cheek. "I hope you do, Lilith. It served your aunt well."

"What do you mean?" She toyed with the bejeweled snake head.

"As you know, Ambeno was a seer," Kukulkan said with a slight smile. "She once told me this bracelet connected her to her purpose, and I hope it does the same for you, Lilith. I must go now. Take care

12

of your father for me. It's not always easy being the oldest in the family." He kissed Lilith on the forehead.

Holding back tears, Lilith wrapped her arms around her uncle's waist. The soft purple fabric of his robe soaked up her tears like a hungry sea sponge. He hugged her back, then reached over and grabbed Segund's hand. He squeezed it so tightly Lilith felt her father jump.

A less threatening tremor broke them apart, signaling it was time to leave.

"Is there a message that you want me to convey to Belial, Segund?"

Her father's lips curled upward, much like the snake's mouth engraved on her bracelet. She shivered at the comparison. "Yes. Tell him that time is not on his side."

Legend of the Timekeepers

1. The Black Land

"You look lost."

Startled, Lilith looked up. A boy, roughly two years older than she, hovered over her. A flat clay disk with what looked like scribbling on it hung from a thin, leather thong around his gritty neck. From his clothes and the color of his skin—a deep olive tone—she knew he was a native of this country—a place her people had aptly named the Black Land because of the dark, rich soil found in the river. Lilith's shoulders sagged. She sighed. What she wouldn't give to see her old, red land again.

"The potter won't be back until it is dark. He's at the market today," the boy said insistently.

Lilith felt her shoulders tense. She had plunked her bottom down under the shade of the potter's workshop, hoping to cool off from this stifling heat. The dryness was starting to take a toll on her skin too. All Lilith wanted now was to be alone in this dreadful place. Perhaps if she ignored the boy, he would disappear.

Suddenly he tugged at one of her crystal hairpieces, almost pulling out her neatly styled blond hair. "Where did you get this?" he asked.

Legend of the Timekeepers

Annoyed, Lilith swatted his hand away as if it was a flying beetle, and stood. "Don't touch that! It's from Atlantis, my homeland!"

The boy stumbled. Lilith pushed her coiled snake bracelet back up her arm for what seemed the millionth time, smoothed out her plain white robe, and clenched her teeth at him.

He laughed. "Your face looks like a date about to pop in the heat. Do you need relief?"

Lilith's jaw dropped. "Relief?"

"Yes, relief. I don't know what you people from Atcha call it. Pass water? Do a dung drop?"

Lilith scratched her slender nose before realizing what this pest was trying to ask her. Then, she smirked. "No. Do you?"

The boy wrinkled his brow. "No. Why would you ask?"

She pointed to what he was wearing—a white linen loincloth held in place by a simple knot on the side. "Because you're wearing that baby's cloth, and by the smell of you, it's about time you change it."

The boy's eyes—the color of tanned leather—grew large. He raked a hand through his short ebony hair before crossing his arms over his glistening chest. "You people from Atcha are all the same, arrogant and ignorant in the ways of my people!"

Lilith blinked. "People from Atcha? I'm from Atlantis."

"Atlantis. Atcha. It makes no difference," he said, shrugging. "At least those of your people who arrived here long before the great flood treat us with respect. At least they attempt to understand and adapt. You recent arrivals seem above us, act better than us."

"We do not!" Lilith stamped her foot. Her woven palm leaf sandal decorated with pearls flew off her foot and landed beside a pile of broken pottery.

In a huff, Lilith limped to retrieve her sandal. She kicked at the pieces of glazed pots and shards of ceramic goblets, fishing around the debris with her sandaled foot. A sudden movement caught her eye. It looked like an insect—a white crawler with eight legs, two front pinching claws, and an odd-shaped tail that curled over its back. Lilith squinted. It was almost the size of her hand and seemed to possess a sharp point on the end of its tail. She was about to kick it when she felt a warm body knock her to the ground. The boy was on top of her, his breathing labored, his skin sticky, yet sweet smelling.

16

"Are you mad, Atcha-girl?"

"I was about to ask you that," Lilith conjured up an appropriate response, "bug-boy!"

He wiped his brow. "My name is Tau, not bug-boy!"

"Humph! Well, my name is Lilith, not Atcha-girl!"

"Do you know what you were about to kick?" He pointed in the direction of the clay debris.

Still a little dazed, she shrugged. "I'm sure you're about to enlighten me."

Tau grunted. "Maybe I shouldn't. You Atchas think you're so smart."

"I'm smart enough to know how to rid myself of a pest like you!" Lilith seethed.

She roughly pushed Tau off her, then stood. Her robe was riddled with dust. She patted herself down while walking toward her orphaned sandal. She noticed that the dumb white crawler with the curled tail had claimed her sandal and was lying on top of it trying to sun itself. Lilith rolled her fingers into the palm of her hands, her long nails cutting into her skin. She was about to raise her foot to stomp on it when she felt one of her hairpins being yanked out from the back of her head. Lilith's fine, fair hair tumbled down just before a gust of wind blew it up into her face to obscure her vision.

Taming her tendrils, she glared around for Tau, who had used her finely crafted crystal hairpin to spear the white crawler through its abdomen and into her sandal. It flailed a moment before giving into its death throes. Tau waved his hand vigorously. When he stopped, Lilith saw that his hand was swelling fast. She noticed Tau's face had changed to a color closer to her lighter skin tone. The hue didn't suit him. It made him sickly looking, drained of life. He stumbled, almost bringing her down, but she held on firm.

"Quick, take me to the Temple Beautiful. Find Istulo. She is a healer, especially in the poisons."

"What are you talking about, Tau? What poison? Only snakes have poison."

Sweat rolled off Tau's temples. His face was now gray, and he was having trouble breathing. "The…the serqet, its tail is full of poison. Quick…take me to the…"

Lilith didn't let Tau finish talking. She propped herself under his arm and swiftly dragged him to the building with the tall marble columns and large palm trees planted in the front—the building Tau

Legend of the Timekeepers

had called the Temple Beautiful. Cutting across the market place, Lilith huffed and puffed until she reached the solid gold doorway. It was etched in symbols foreign to her. She hoped this Istulo, or whatever name Tau had muttered, was inside. She banged on the door, once, twice, three times before someone answered. A boy—correction—a man with sea green eyes, golden hair, high cheekbones, and skin like hers answered the door. He was dressed like an initiate—in a pale green robe and matching headband. He smiled at Lilith. She shyly smiled back. Then, she remembered why she was there.

"I...I need Istulo. Now!" Lilith commanded. "Tau's been stung by a ser... a ser..." She tried to remember what Tau had called it. Her mind was fluff, and she shook her head to clear it.

"Do you mean a serqet?" the handsome young man asked.

She nodded her head vigorously. "Yes, that's it! Please, he needs Istulo to heal him!"

"Take him over to those embroidered benches. I'll tell Istulo. She'll bring the appropriate antidote."

Before Lilith could ask him for some assistance, he sprinted down a marble hallway with odd-shaped, colorful pictographs of foreign gods and goddesses drawn across the walls. Flecks of glittering metal—much like the color of orichalcum—were embedded in the tiles on the floor. Strangely, this place felt like home to Lilith, even though she knew that that part of her life was gone forever. Her stomach twinged recalling that she had only been ten at the time of Atlantis's sinking.

It was hard to believe she and Father had landed in the Black Land almost six moons ago. It had been a dangerous, harrowing journey traveling away from the dark, ash-filled sky, drifting for many moon phases while relying on fish and whatever supplies the ship had for sustenance, while waiting for the water-covered lands to open up again. Father had told her the Children of the Law of One had foreseen the rain and the darkness, and that they should be prepared with enough food, clothing, and supplies to endure the trip. All would be cleared up, Father had shared with her, and the lands would be revealed soon. Then, Atlanteans would be given a second chance at a new life in new places throughout the Earth.

She sat Tau down on the soft bench cushions and propped him against the elaborately decorated wall. His whole body was now

18

Sharon Ledwith

dripping wet, his lips were dry, and his breathing ragged. "Stay with me, Tau," she whispered. "Istulo is coming."

A group of priests and priestesses passed by them, seemingly in quiet debate. As in Atlantis, all were dressed in the appropriate colored robes—some in pale green indicating they were novices like the young man who greeted her at the door, and some in light blue, distinguishing them as more advanced in their training. Lilith noticed no one in that group wore any white silk garments, which were reserved for only the highest ranking orders of priesthood. From a corridor down the opposite way, Lilith heard the musical sound of crystal bowls being played. The harmonious pitch was enchanting, making her heart beat faster and chest open wider. Suddenly, Lilith could feel her crystal hairpins vibrate to meet the higher frequency, and her whole body started to respond to this wonderful resonance.

Tau moaned something incoherent—maybe a phrase from his culture—then started to choke. Lilith's mouth went dry and she stood up to run, almost smacking into an old, wizen woman standing in front of her. Lilith grabbed the woman by the arms, hoping she didn't break any of her brittle bones, to stop the old woman from falling. Their eyes locked. A gauzy film, the color of curdling milk, coated both the woman's eyes, while a mass of wrinkles seemed to be the only thing keeping her eyes in their sockets. Lifeless, white hair was held in place by an orichalcum headband, hair Lilith thought that must have been thick and luxurious at one time.

"Do let me go, young Lilith, I won't break, you know," she wheezed.

Startled, Lilith let go, and the old woman straightened up as best as she could muster. Her gown was of the finest silk, all white and radiant, and smooth to the touch. *Robes of a Priestess of the Highest Order*, Lilith thought.

"Move aside, so that I may attend to your friend," the old priestess said.

"Um, Tau's not really my friend, he's just a…"

She held up a bony hand to silence Lilith. "You must care about him. You brought him to me."

"Yes, but, it was an accident. You see, Tau killed this…ser…white crawler with a stinger tail using one of my hair…"

"A serqet, Lilith," the old priestess corrected as she pulled a small ceramic vial out of the metal-flaked pouch attached to the

19

Legend of the Timekeepers

white sash around her thin waist. "And there are no accidents. All is as it should be."

The old priestess was starting to creep Lilith out. *No accidents? All is as it should be?* Her stomach started to ache. She couldn't stop the dark memories from searing through her mind as she relived the destruction of her homeland, watching everything she knew disappear from the safety of their southbound ship. The loud bang. Thick, dark spiraling smoke. A brown-black sky. No moon, no stars, no sun. Cold, sour air. The relentless rain. The roaring gales. The flooded lands. It was all too much. They had gotten away only by the grace of Poseidon.

Her fingers curled into her palms, and she winced at the tender spots she had recently cut into. Lilith cleared her throat. "How can you say that? What happened in Atlantis was not how it should be. Those people, my people, shouldn't have been made to suffer and die like that!"

The old priestess made a sound like a small animal dying. She wiped the sweat from Tau's brow, his ebony hair now flat and damp, and opened his mouth with two spindly fingers. She pulled out the wooden stopper from the vial and carefully poured the liquid into his mouth. "You're naïve if you think your fellow Atlanteans didn't deserve what they got. You give out, you get back. The only people left on Atlantis when it crumbled into nothingness were those who went against the teachings of the Children of the Law of One. In your heart, you know this. The Sons of Belial deserved worse for choosing to worship ease and pleasure over love and kindness."

Before Lilith could reply, Tau moaned, coughed, then lunged forward. The old priestess held him by the shoulders while his breathing became easier. She giggled—almost sounding child-like—and then gently stroked the back of his neck. Then she checked over Tau's hand. Lilith noticed the swelling had gone down considerably, leaving only a small, red puncture mark to attest to Tau's misfortune. "You'll be fine, Tau. You are lucky you have a friend in Lilith."

Tau snorted. "She is not my friend, Istulo. She's as vengeful as the serqet."

Lilith's eyes widened. So this broken-down old woman was Istulo? Somehow, Lilith felt mildly disappointed, like she was expecting someone grander, more auspicious-looking. She frowned.

20

Sharon Ledwith

Istulo pinched his neck and held firm. "You need to decide who you would rather be stung by—a creature of habit or a creature of nature?"

"Do I have another choice?" Tau asked, gritting his teeth.

Istulo raised a grizzled brow. "There are always choices, Tau. You need to remember that you must live with your choices and no one else's. But before you make your choice, remember that habits can be broken, but nature is one's true essence. So, which do you choose—the serqet or Lilith?"

Tau smirked. Lilith rolled her eyes. *He must be feeling better.*

"Perhaps he needs to feel the sting of my tongue," Lilith said curtly.

Tau grinned. "Believe me, I already have."

Her whole body straightened, then she threw back her head and laughed. It was the first time she had laughed like that in a long time. She didn't even care if her long hair was unbound, it felt freeing, like she had given herself permission to be five years old again.

"Feels good doesn't it, Lilith?" Istulo asked.

Catching her breath, Lilith nodded greedily. Then, she straightened. "Hey, how do you know my name? We've never met before, have we?"

"Have we?" Istulo asked Lilith, a trace of a smile chased her lips.

"I'm sure I would remember you," Lilith replied, shrugging. "Are you from Atlantis?"

Her bristly chin moved slightly. "Yes, once, long ago. Another lifetime I suppose. I've moved to many places, learned many things, especially in the healing arts. This is where I have decided to root myself and teach what I know. This is where I will die."

There was a hint of sadness and maybe regret in Istulo's voice, but she still hadn't answered Lilith properly. Lilith decided to dig deeper. "Do you know my father, Segund?"

Istulo fell silent for a moment before she answered. "Your father is the Keeper of the seventh Arch of Atlantis, yes?"

Lilith raised a fair brow. "Yes."

"I met with him almost three moon phases ago. Your father has been very worried about you since you've arrived here. He told me you haven't made a single friend or even picked up a scroll to read. So I suggested to him that I do a life reading for you to help you move forward with your new life."

Legend of the Timekeepers

Tau guffawed. "I would love to see what occupation you come up with for her!"

Lilith glared at Tau. "Be careful. I'm sure I can round up more of those ser...white crawlers."

"How hard is it for you people to say 'serqet'?" Tau asked in exasperation.

Lilith ignored him and turned to Istulo. "What is a life reading?"

Istulo pulled a small ceramic disk from her metallic pouch. "This is called a life seal, Lilith. Right now it is blank, but when I've had a chance to assess you based on your karmic development, this will help you decide on your lifetime occupation."

Lilith stared at the disk as if it were a white crawler. She wrinkled her nose. "How?"

Istulo reached out to touch Lilith's cheek, just as a sudden, sharp twinge rippled across the old priestess's face. She withdrew her hand and said, "Through the inscriptions I write on this disk during a self-induced trance. I listen to the internal guidance given and record this advice. The results of this transaction then become your life seal."

Tau grinned. "It'll probably still be blank after the trance."

"Have you ever had a life reading, Tau?" Lilith asked, curling her fingers.

"Yes," Istulo answered for him. "He received his life seal before the great flood made us take refuge on higher ground until the waters receded. Tau proudly wears his seal around his neck." Then Istulo picked up the empty ceramic vial and deposited it in her pouch. "I must take my leave and attend to my new students. Lilith, I trust I will see you on the next new moon for your life reading. Do not be late."

It sounded more like a demand than a request to Lilith. She nodded in response.

Istulo trundled down the hall toward the area where Lilith had heard the crystal bowls being played. Confident that the old priestess was out of listening range, Lilith screwed her full lips to one side and turned to face Tau. "So, what's your lifetime occupation supposed to be, Tau? A farmer? A baker? A dung-ditch maker?"

Seemingly unfazed, Tau reached for his life seal, held it out like it was a piece of sweet fruit to taunt Lilith with, and said, "I am to be a special scribe to an important emissary."

Sharon Ledwith

Lilith pushed her creeping fair locks off the side of her face, but it seemed a losing battle. Her hair was starting to feel like straw. She sputtered her lips and said, "The only scribes I've seen around here record the farmer's crop share. Correct me if I'm wrong but that doesn't sound very special to me."

Tau's face fell. "No. But you wait and see. Istulo's life readings are never wrong!"

Lilith stamped her foot against a polished tile with enough force to knock her remaining sandal off. This time the sandal smacked a man across the top of his back as he attempted to leave the Temple Beautiful.

Lilith covered her mouth. So far this day, her sandals had gotten her into nothing but trouble. *First the white crawler, now this.* She removed her hand and flashed him an apologetic smile. "I…I am so sorry," Lilith stammered. "It was an accident."

The man turned around and stared at Lilith. His body was draped over a golden walking stick decorated with pearls and various gems. The man appeared old but not as wrinkled and gaunt as Istulo. There was still life in his wild, white hair, which stuck out every which way and needed a good brushing. His eyes were the color of the desert sand, and his skin the color of alabaster. The gown he wore was deep blue, marking him as a sage. He smiled at Lilith a good long moment, making her feel as if she was being assessed by a hardened teacher. Slowly, he reached for her sandal by his bare foot, picked it up, and held it out to Lilith.

"Young lady—" he said smiling "—there are no accidents."

Legend of the Timekeepers

2. The Temple Beautiful

*L*ilith nervously tapped her palm sandal against the shimmering tiles outside the entrance to Istulo's chambers in the Temple Beautiful. She had arrived early, as requested, catching the lingering scent of perfumed incense and hearing the methodic tones of priests and priestesses in morning meditation. A pair of entwined serpents, carved out of black marble and trimmed with gold, adorned the top of Istulo's doorway in a threatening manner. Both serpents stared down at her, their sculpted tongues and fangs emerging from open jaws as if ready to consume whoever dared walk past them. Lilith shuddered, feeling like she was back in bed with the snake her uncle had attempted to give her. She stopped tapping and took a few steps back, almost knocking over a crystal vase on a white marble pillar. Turning, Lilith grabbed it in time before it fell. Taking a deep breath, she placed the vase back on its shining perch, then wiped away the strands of hair clinging to her forehead.

"A little oil mixed with powdered sandalwood will tame your hair," the girl behind Lilith blurted.

Jolted, Lilith turned around to glare at the girl who obviously had no manners. Lilith's eyes were immediately drawn to her shoulder-length thick, red hair. It was braided in rows that tapered down into

Legend of the Timekeepers

fine points. Small seashells decorated the end of each braid as if they had been carefully selected for such a purpose. The girl's red hair wasn't the same as Lilith's Uncle Kukulkan's cinnamon shade. Instead, the girl possessed a bright strawberry hue, the likes Lilith had never seen before. It was distracting yet mesmerizing at the same time.

The girl cupped Lilith's chin and nudged it down. Wide green eyes, the color of a sea turtle, glared at Lilith. "My mother says it's rude to stare."

Lilith's nostrils flared. "Well, my mother—" She cut herself off, feeling the void in her heart from the loss of her mother, then continued, "—taught me to offer advice only when asked for it. And I don't recall asking for your advice about my hair."

"Suit yourself." She shrugged. "But if you want to get rid of that frizzy, fly-away look, take my advice—sandalwood oil works wonders. Oh, and while you're at it, you should add some accessories to your plain white gown. It will not only enhance the color of your beautiful blue eyes, it will bring to life whatever you're wearing."

Lilith started to cross her arms over her chest, then stopped herself. "What kind of accessories?"

The girl smiled as if she'd found a lost treasure. Her teeth were pearl with a hint of pink. She rubbed her hands together briskly, and said, "An embroidered sash to show off your hips, and a seashell and pearl necklace to enhance your neckline. Your snake bracelet is a definite keeper, but use only one crystal hairpin—not five—and preferably purple or blue. You want your hair to move naturally, not be held back. Oh, wait, one more thing."

Lilith's face twitched. "Just one?"

The girl pointed to Lilith's feet. "Palm-woven sandals are out of style. And where's your satchel?"

"I…I don't have one."

The girl thumbed her square chin. "That's an easy fix, I have loads of them—I'll lend you one that will pull your outfit together. You'll have a suitor in no time."

"A suitor?"

The girl nodded just enough to show off her dangling bead earrings. Lilith must have counted at least five different seashell bracelets running up each arm. The girl's white sheath had beaded straps instead of cloth straps and a herringbone design ran along the gown's bottom. A belt dyed a deep purple hugged the girl's waist and allowed for her hips to flare out in an attractive way. Curious, Lilith lowered her head to see what kind of sandals were in style. Lilith's eyes widened. Spotted animal-skin sandals with a heel at least as long as Lilith's middle finger adorned the girl's feet. Lilith blinked, feeling the need to slink into a nest of white crawlers.

"Yes, a suitor," the girl said in exasperation. "A woman is not complete without a man."

"So what you're saying—" Lilith inclined her head "—is that all this accessorizing is to attract a mate?"

The girl rolled her eyes. "Yes, that's the point of it."

Lilith giggled. "If that's the case, you must have a boatload of suitors to choose from."

The girl's face fell. Her normal skin tone was close to Lilith's but a little more tanned. Then a group of young, native men passed them in the hallway of the Temple Beautiful where Lilith been waiting to see Istulo. Lilith thought they might be artists by the way all their hands were speckled with blue, green, and yellow paint. And all of them wore linen loincloths, like Tau. They stared at the red-headed girl for a moment, then laughed and cut a wide berth around her.

"Freak," one of the men muttered.

"Fancy her?" another artist asked.

"Shave her head, and I'll think about it."

The group guffawed, slapping the man on his back, while they turned down a corridor.

"What was that all about?" Lilith asked, feeling a sudden drop inside her.

The girl didn't answer Lilith. She was too busy looking inside a spotted animal-skin satchel which matched her sandals perfectly. She pulled out something Lilith recognized—a life seal. The girl stared at the disk as if it held a long-awaited answer to a question she'd asked one too many times.

"Why are you here?" Lilith asked. "You've already got your life seal."

"I have more questions for Istulo." She continued to stare at the disk.

Lilith sighed. "My name is Lilith. What's your name?"

Her shoulders relaxed slightly. A hint of a smile broke out on her face. Her upturned nose wiggled. "She-Aba. I was born here in the

Legend of the Timekeepers

Black Land. Both my parents arrived from Atlantis fourteen years ago yesterday. My mother gave birth to me the next day."

Lilith perked up. "That would make today your birthday!"

She-Aba beamed. "Yes. That's why I'm here. For my birthday last year, I had my life reading done by Istulo. But recently, there's been a hiccup in my plans. It's like my life seal rearranged itself, and now I'm confused. I'm here for a reaffirmation."

"What's the problem?"

She-Aba traced her life seal with the tip of her perfectly shaped fingernail. "My lifetime occupation was supposed to be to design clothing for the people of the various positions in the court and temples."

Lilith smirked. "That makes perfect sense."

"I know, right? So why, all of a sudden, would my life seal change from designing clothing to something completely different?"

Lilith arched a fair brow. "How different?"

"Well, instead of clothing people in lavish robes and gowns for others to appreciate, the seal suggests that I'll be doing the opposite by covering up and hiding the truth. I don't understand it at all. I thought my life was all planned out for me."

"I thought mine was too, until my country blew up and slid into the ocean," Lilith muttered.

"Hey, look at the bright side, at least your hair isn't red like mine."

Lilith eyed She-Aba carefully. "What's wrong with red hair? My uncle has red hair and it suits him fine."

She-Aba moved in closer. "If you haven't noticed already, there aren't many redheads around here. The natives think red is magical, and anyone with red hair is considered a freak of nature."

"That's ridiculous!" Lilith said loud enough to cause an echo down the marble hallway. "Is that the reason why those artists were rude to you? Because you have red hair?"

"Red is a very powerful color," a raspy voice said from behind both girls.

Lilith and She-Aba jumped. They slowly turned to find Istulo hovering over them.

Wearing the same white gown and orichalcum headband Lilith saw her dressed in before, Istulo nodded slightly before she said, "Red represents the essence of life—if we are drained of blood, we are drained of energy. The people of the Black Land understand this, and therefore red is reserved only for their gods and goddesses."

Lilith giggled. "Don't tell She-Aba that, she'll think she's a goddess."

She-Aba poked her in the ribs, but Lilith ignored her and continued to giggle.

Istulo squinted at She-Aba. "Did we have a session together?"

She-Aba licked her pink lips. "No, Istulo. I was hoping, since it's my birthday, that I could get you to look at my life seal and reaffirm it for me. It's changed since last year."

Istulo scrunched her weathered face, which made her appear gaunt. "Life seals represent the outer expression of your inner development and are binding contracts with your soul. They do not change, She-Aba."

"Mine did," She-Aba said, shrugging.

Istulo held out her spindly hand. "Let me see it."

She-Aba passed Istulo her ceramic life seal. The old priestess brought it close to her eyes and touched it with a thin, gnarled finger. She wheezed once and fell silent for what seemed an eternity, all the while tapping her finger upon the disk like she was beating on a tiny drum. Then Istulo started chanting. At first it was soft, but as she progressed it got louder and louder until Lilith had to cover her ears. A lioness in heat sounded better than her caterwauling.

Suddenly, Istulo stopped. She handed She-Aba back her life seal. "There is illusion and deception indicated."

She-Aba's eyes bugged. "But...what about designing beautiful clothing for people in the court and temples?"

"That is for you to intuit, She-Aba. All I can tell you is that your lifetime occupation has shifted. You must accept this as higher guidance."

She-Aba took the small disk from Istulo. Her pert lips started to quiver. "Shifted? You're telling me my whole life plan has...has shifted?"

With a face void of expression, Istulo nodded. "It would appear so. Now go. Study your new plan. Learn it. Accept it."

"But..." She-Aba begged.

Istulo held up her wrinkled hand. "Your time with me is over. I have an appointment for a life reading with Lilith. Either go to the

Legend of the Timekeepers

meditation room for insight from the Shining Serpent, or leave the Temple Beautiful. It is your choice, She-Aba."

Lilith could almost feel She-Aba's anguish. She had her heart set on being a clothing designer. In the short time she had known She-Aba, Lilith had seen she had a flare for clothing and accessorizing people. Before She-Aba turned on her spotted animal-skin heels, Lilith grabbed her by the shoulder and whispered in her ear, "If your life seal can change, than that means it can change again. Don't worry. We'll figure this out. Together."

Without turning around, She-Aba gently touched Lilith's hand and whispered, "Thank you, Lilith. You're the best birthday gift I've ever received."

Sharon Ledwith

3. The Snake Charmer

L ilith sat off in a corner of the marketplace, out of the sun, thinking about her life reading. Brilliant colors of blue, turquoise, and yellow linens were carefully draped over every merchant's booth to protect them, and their wares, from the sun's relentless rays. She tried to drown out the sound of children laughing and screaming, but it was no use. Then, she tried to lose herself within the sea of distraction, but that was even more distracting.. Deciding that a walk around the market would do her good, Lilith stood up. She brushed down her linen sheath, complete with a deep blue sash and matching sandals compliments of She-Aba, and walked towards the west, away from the glaring rays, towards the alluring smell of incense.

A small linen satchel—the color of coral—hung over her shoulder. Lilith adjusted her new shell and bead necklace—another addition from She-Aba—as she poked about, inspecting each merchant's area like she was searching for a clue or answer to the meaning of her life reading. Slipping her slender hand into her satchel, she fished around until she felt the small ceramic disk that had changed her life and shifted her perception.

Legend of the Timekeepers

Slowly, she pulled out her life seal and looked it over as if it were something she was deciding to purchase at the market. She flared her nostrils and emitted a small guttural sound from the back of her throat. If she had had a choice—which according to Istulo, she did not—Lilith would toss her life seal into the deepest part of the river and let the current carry it into the sea. Her fist engulfed the small disk.

A Timekeeper? This is my lifetime occupation? What does that even mean? Lilith thought. She grumbled while pushing her snake bracelet up over her wrist. "Time is not something one can keep!" she blurted.

A native merchant and his wife sitting on a wide reed mat looked up at Lilith strangely and offered her a date to sample. She apologetically smiled, reached for the dried brown fruit, and popped it into her mouth. Its sweetness pacified her, and she let the warm date slide down her throat. "Thank you. I'll take a handful for my father."

The man, who was close in age to Lilith's father, flashed a toothless grin. His skin was leathery, and he wore a long loincloth that reached the top of his knees. He motioned for his wife, who wore a white sheath dotted with brown spots, to package the dates in a palm leaf. Lilith bent to place her life seal on the reed mat in front of the man so she could look through her satchel for a piece of silver to give to the merchant when she heard him make the sound of a baby monkey.

He held up his hand. "No. Dates are gift. You take."

Lilith stopped searching through her satchel. She looked down at the merchant, who was busy staring at her life seal. His mouth was open, and he nudged his wife.

"Are…are you sure?"

The merchant's wife quickly bundled up the dates and held them up for Lilith. "Yes. Ra protects you. Take dates. It is gift."

Lilith shrugged. She gingerly took the wrapped dates, slid them into her satchel, and then started to walk away until she felt a rough hand grasp her ankle. She looked down to find the merchant's wife staring up at her. "Wait. Forgot life seal. Bad for fate. Must take with you, keep with you."

Lilith pursed her lips. It wouldn't have bothered her one bit to lose her life seal. But it meant something to the natives. Maybe these people could help her figure out what a Timekeeper was. She

32

smiled as the woman released her foot, then squatted to retrieve her life seal, still on the reed mat. She licked her dry lips, then looked the merchant in his dark, brown eyes. "What does this mean?" she asked, shaking the small disk in front of him as if she had something to sell to him. "And what does your god, Ra, have to do with it?"

The man wiped away the sweat building on his balding head. He glanced at his wife, who was nervously chewing her bottom lip, and then back to Lilith. "Take dates. It is to thank Ra. You will see."

"They can't tell you, Atcha-girl. You have to figure it out for yourself."

Lilith cringed. She squeezed her life seal, wishing it would crumble, but it was stronger than she thought. She knew that annoying, pesky voice. "Hello, Tau," she said coolly. "What's the matter, couldn't find any white crawlers to slay?"

Tau laughed. "You're still having problems pronouncing some of our words. Maybe I should teach you since I'm to be a scribe."

Lilith stood up and turned to face Tau. He wore a fresher loincloth with a small leather satchel fastened to the side of it. He also appeared to have gotten his hair washed and cut, which curled perfectly around his ears. Tau still displayed his life seal around his neck as if he were a peacock showing off his plumes. She smirked. "What's the occasion? Found a girl that would put up with you?"

"It's market day. Father insists I look my best."

"Well, if that's your best, I'll have to introduce you to a friend of mine. She has a flare with colors and fabrics. Maybe you should give her a try."

Tau wrinkled his brow. "What's wrong with what I am wearing? It's cool and allows my skin to breathe. You Atchas will learn soon enough about how to dress for the desert!"

"Hey, She-Aba has given me—"

"Did you say She-Aba?" Tau interrupted.

"Yes, why?"

Tau snorted. "She's...she's odd, a freak. She pretends to be important, like our gods."

Lilith set her jaw. "Says who? Your people and their silly rules?"

"Red is reserved for our gods and goddesses only," Tau said, flailing his arms. "To try to resemble them in any way is unnatural and is forbidden. To wear red takes away the power of the gods who take away power from people in revenge. It brings severe consequences to those who mock our ways."

Legend of the Timekeepers

"She-Aba was born that way!" Lilith shouted. "She's not mocking you or your ways! She's just being who she's supposed to be!" Then, with a force she'd never felt before, Lilith threw her life seal at Tau's head. He ducked in time.

The small ceramic disk rolled through the marketplace and smacked against the side of a cream-colored basket with a lid on it. Flustered, and ignoring the stares she received from the other merchants and their customers, Lilith pushed Tau aside. "Guess I'd better go collect my silly life seal, or the gods will put a curse on me!"

Lilith strutted through the market like she owned it. She became aware of Tau racing after her. "Go away, Tau, there's no white crawlers around for you to protect me from!"

"But, Lilith, wait for me!" Tau cried. "Stop!"

Fat chance of that. Lilith reached the woven basket decorated with heads of hooded serpents. She grimaced at the pictures and looked around for her life seal. It was lodged under the basket, so without consideration for the basket's owner, she gave it a hard kick. The lid popped off the moment the basket hit the earth. An odd sound erupted from the basket, and she walked around to see what it might be. Suddenly, a long snake emerged from the basket, hissing at anything around it.

Lilith froze in place. Sweat blistered through her skin. Her heart raced, her mouth went dry, and she held her legs tightly together so she would not relieve herself in front of the crowd. Tau stopped his advances. She could hear his labored breathing. It almost matched hers, only she could feel her chest closing up and her head getting lighter. The snake rose to the height of Lilith's waist and hissed at her. The sensation of its putrid breath crawling across her bare arms made her skin ripple and her body shake. She closed her eyes, knowing that somehow this was Tau's gods' retribution for what she had just said. Then, Lilith heard a flute being played behind her. It sounded lulling and calming, her whole body relaxed instantly.

She opened her eyes. The flute player was now beside her. Lilith glanced over and gasped. It was the handsome young man who had greeted her at the door of the Temple Beautiful. A green sheath with flecks of gold covered his muscular body, and she noticed he was absent of his headband, but wore a life seal around his neck like Tau. Sweat trickled down his lean arms as he continued to play. His blond hair was neatly pulled back and held in place with a purple crystal. She reached up to touch her own purple crystal hairpin, which neatly bound her hair in one place. She caught a whiff of sandalwood oil—her new best friend, now that it tamed her hair in this arid climate.

"Don't move, Lilith," Tau whispered from behind her.

"What's he doing?" Lilith asked quietly, using her chin as a guide.

"He's bewitching the cobra. Mica is what is called a snake charmer," Tau murmured.

Lilith's eyes widened. "You know him!"

The snake hissed, and its hood flared.

The snake charmer named Mica stopped playing and glared at Lilith. Even while he showed displeasure, she found no flaws in his beautiful face. She grinned sheepishly at him.

He rolled his eyes, tossed his flute to Tau, and pushed Lilith out of the way in time before the snake lashed out at her. Then Mica jumped to the reptile's side, moving his hands rapidly around the snake, not giving him anything to aim at. He darted around the snake, going in circles, following the sun's patterns, bobbing his body up and down, side to side, always moving his hands in front of the snake's hissing face. Lilith heard the flute trill and squeak as Tau blew on it. She winced as Mica swiftly grasped the snake's head, its tail wreathing and wrapping around one of his legs. He reached for the open basket on the ground, sat it upright, untwined the snake's tail from his leg, and eased the snake back into the basket, all the while making clicking sounds with his tongue.

"In you go, Kheti." He gently patted the lid of the basket. "You'll get your supper of mice later."

Lilith heard the snake hiss one last time before the crowd broke out in cheers. A few merchants bowed before Mica and offered him pomegranates, grapes, melons, fish, swathes of fabric, and finely-crafted baskets. Most gave Lilith a stare that would have destroyed Atlantis all over again. She averted her eyes, but it didn't help. Everyone seemed to be blaming her for what could have resulted in someone getting hurt or killed.

"Why don't you ever listen?" Tau wagged the flute at her. "I told you to wait. You didn't. I told you to stop. You didn't. Do you have a death wish?"

Lilith could feel her eyes well up with tears. She shook her head. "I...I don't know. I just want to go home."

Legend of the Timekeepers

Tau sighed loud enough for Lilith to hear. "I will take you home. You live by the Temple of Sacrifice, next to the houses of the temple staff, right?"

Her shoulders sagged. "No. Home to Atlantis."

Then, Tau started playing the flute. It was worse than Istulo's chanting. He couldn't hold a tune if his life depended on it. Lilith covered her ears and glared at Tau. He stopped playing. "You seemed so sad. I thought I'd try to cheer you up."

Tau sounded so serious, she couldn't help but giggle. "Cheer me up, or strike me down?"

"That noise would kill my cobra," a young man said behind Lilith.

Lilith glanced over her shoulder. It was Mica. His tanned arms were full of the gifts he'd received from the grateful merchants. He passed a pomegranate to her and a melon to Tau. "Trade you, Tau."

Tau handed Mica his flute for the melon. He thumped the round fruit to check for freshness.

"How come you didn't mention that you knew Tau the day we met at the Temple Beautiful?" Lilith asked, juggling the pomegranate between her hands.

Mica raised a fair brow. "We've met?"

Lilith felt her cheeks heat up. She dropped the fruit. Mica caught it before it hit the ground. "You're right, Tau, this one is clumsy."

Tau had already started digging into his melon. "Mmm? Oh yes, and she pronounces our language as if she has a handful of live clams in her mouth."

"I'm with her on that matter," Mica said, grinning. "Some of your words leave my tongue tied."

"Exactly," Lilith blurted. "That white crawler with the stinger tail, um a ser—"

"Serqet," Mica finished for her. "Yes, I know what you mean. It's a totally different dialect."

Lilith pointed at Mica. "Precisely!"

"Are you two finished making fun of my people?" Tau asked with a mouthful of melon.

"No," Mica replied. "What about you, Lilith?"

"Nope," Lilith answered. Then her eyes widened. "Hey, you do know me."

Mica shrugged. "How could I not. You're the talk of the Temple Beautiful."

36

Sharon Ledwith

Lilith balked. "I…I am?"

"That's what I've heard through some of the students. And Istulo seems to like you too."

"S-She…she does?"

"I think Lilith's also developed a stutter. Now she'll never say our words properly," Tau said.

Lilith reached over and shoved a chunk of melon in Tau's mouth. Mica laughed, then handed Lilith back her pomegranate and winked at her. Startled, and not knowing how to react, her heart flipped-flopped as she said, "Um, that was amazing, what you did with the snake."

"Thank you. I earn my supper here at the market with my cobra Kheti and learn all I can at the Temple Beautiful. I was recently accepted as a novice to study to be a healer. I know I have many years of training ahead of me, but it will be well worth it."

"How long have you lived in the Black Land?" Lilith asked, juggling the piece of fruit again.

"Long enough to learn how to pronounce serqet," he replied, grinning. "But to answer your question, I was about eight when I arrived."

Lilith nodded, trying to figure out his age in her head. Close to Tau, maybe a year older, she guessed. She decided to fish more. "Do you live with your parents still?"

Mica's clean-shaven face lost all expression. "My family is gone. All assassinated by the followers of the Sons of Belial. There was nothing left for me in Atlantis, so I left on a trader's ship. The Black Land was his final stop so I made it my home. It was Istulo who gave me shelter, allowed me into the Temple Beautiful, and finally asked one of the priests to accept me as a student of the healing arts."

Lilith squeezed the pomegranate so hard it burst all over her white sheath. She heard Tau gasp and mutter something about being clumsy. Red dots splattered all over her as if she'd been attacked by an army of white crawlers. She sighed, dropping the fruit. It didn't even have the chance to hit the ground before a bird swooped down and claimed it. Lilith jumped out of the way and into Mica's already full arms.

Mica fell backwards and landed about an arm's length away from his snake's basket. Lilith, knowing her face now matched the color of She-Aba's hair, tried to push herself off of Mica before Tau

37

Legend of the Timekeepers

opened his mouth to say something about her awkwardness. Then she spied it. Her life seal was a finger's length away from Mica's ear. She smiled. She needed a good distraction. Reaching over, Lilith scooped up the small ceramic disk.

Her hand was engulfed in mid-air by Mica. "What's this?"

"Um, my life seal," she replied, curling her toes. "I…I threw it at Tau in a fit of anger but missed him, and it rolled over here."

Mica stared at her life seal for a moment, as if mesmerized by it; entranced. Lilith thought that odd—the snake charmer was being charmed. She peeked at his own life seal lying on his glistening chest, and her eyes widened. *He has spirals on his life seal too!* Then, she spotted the coiled serpents also etched upon it, and frowned.

"There are spirals on your life seal." Mica broke his silence and loosened the grip he had upon her hand. "Is your father the Keeper of the seventh Arch of Atlantis by chance?"

Lilith rolled off of Mica, managing to keep her distance from the basket. She stood, looked down at him and nodded. "Yes. Why?"

His face had changed again. It appeared darker, akin to the moon losing its glow. "Because, according to my life seal, it seems—" he started to say as he stood. Mica brushed himself off before continuing, "—that we are to be mortal enemies."

4. The Seventh Arch of Atlantis

"It could be worse," She-Aba said in a consoling tone.

"Worse than mortal enemies?" Lilith sighed. "I don't see how."

"Sure. He could have been a redhead." She-Aba grinned.

Lilith opened her mouth to reply, then burst out laughing instead.

"Lilith," Segund said, entering her bed chambers.

She stopped laughing enough to wipe her mouth. "Yes, Father?"

"I'm going to enter the seventh Arch of Atlantis to receive insight from the Children of the Law of One. I must finish documenting Atlantis's history to store inside the Guardian of the Sands before it is unveiled in seven days time." He smiled, creating lines of happiness around his eyes. "It's nice to hear you laugh again."

Lilith rolled off her bed, the silkiness of her purple sheets making the task easier. She walked over to him, adjusted his linen shirt, and tugged on his full, gold-hued beard. "You look tired, Father. Your hair is a mess, and your beard is scraggly. Maybe you should rest."

Legend of the Timekeepers

She-Aba jumped off the other side of Lilith's bed. "Ohhh, let me do your hair, Segund! I know the perfect blend of oils to use. And while we're at it, I'll braid your beard for you, too!"

Segund's nostrils flared. "Perhaps another day, She-Aba, when time permits."

"You should listen to She-Aba, Father. After all, it only took her a short time to do this for me," Lilith said, opening her arms wide and spinning around.

A breeze coming from the open porch made the blue gown she wore billow and flutter. A white seashell belt hugged her waist, and a pair of palm-woven sandals accented with pearls and colored crystals covered her feet. She-Aba had even managed to tame her hair with lavender oil and an assortment of clear crystal pins. Her orichalcum snake bracelet crept down her forearm to imprison her slim wrist. Lilith stopped spinning, pushed up her bracelet, placed her palms together, and bowed to her father.

Segund clapped. "Very nice, She-Aba. I may take you up on your offer, yet."

She-Aba snatched a thick leather belt with stitched on spiked-metal disks from a pile of clothing on the floor, next to her overnight satchel. "At least make yourself presentable for the Children of the Law of One, Segund." She padded over on bare feet and fastened the belt around his waist.

He rolled his eyes. "Fine, She-Aba, but make it quick."

She pulled at his shirt and a small, tan book fell out of the waistband of his deep blue pants. She-Aba dove to retrieve it. "What's this?"

"That is my record keeper. It is what I use to scribe the messages I receive from the Law of One."

"It's beautifully crafted," She-Aba whispered, running her finger down the length of its black spine. "Why is there a gold Eye of Ra pressed onto the front cover? I didn't think people from Atlantis worshipped our gods."

"Actually, we call that the Eye of One," Segund said, procuring the book from her. "And, trust me when I tell you, our beliefs don't stray far from your beliefs."

"How far have you gotten in documenting our history, Father?"

She-Aba resumed her primping, tugging hard on the belt. Segund flinched. "Only the last one hundred years, before the first major earthquake took a great deal of our land." Then he frowned. "During the time of Belial's reign."

"Will you be late to bed?" Lilith watched She-Aba adjust some of the metal disks.

"Most likely, Lilith," he replied, pulling at his shirt. "Do not wait up for me."

She-Aba slapped his hand. "No, Segund, you'll ruin the look."

Lilith giggled. "Father's not going away in body, only in mind."

"A well-dressed body accentuates a well-trained mind." She-Aba snapped her fingers. "It's all about presentation."

"No, She-Aba, it's all about preservation." Segund tweaked her nose. "And that is precisely what I'm going to do—preserve Atlantis's memories. Good night, girls, and do not stay up too late."

Segund winked at Lilith and She-Aba, then turned on his sandals and left the room.

"You really are good with making people look their best," Lilith said, watching her father leave. "I still can't believe your lifetime occupation has shifted. Has your life seal revealed anything to you?"

She-Aba sighed. "No. Not yet. But I'm determined to change it back. I can't see myself doing anything else, so I will fake it until I make it so. What about yours?"

Lilith's shoulders slumped. "Nothing since we talked last by the fountain. I'm still supposed to be a Timekeeper."

"Atcha-girl!" a voice called from outside.

Lilith jumped.

She-Aba's eyes widened. "Who's that?"

There was only one person who called her by that name. Lilith twisted her lips as if she'd eaten something disgusting. "Tau."

"The goat farmer's son from the market? The boy who walks around like a rooster?"

"Is there any other?"

"Lilith?" Tau called again. "I know you're in there. Your room is lit up with glowing crystals and I can smell incense burning."

Lilith groaned. She padded over to the balcony and peered over. "What is it, bug-boy?"

She-Aba looked down too. She waved. "Hello, Tau." Then she frowned. "Don't you ever wear anything bright? Your schenti is so plain."

Tau looked down at his attire. Lilith looked too. Usually Tau wore a loincloth, but tonight, he wore a pleated loin skirt that

41

reached the top of his knees and was fastened in the front by a plain, thin belt. Hanging from his belt was a small, leather pouch. His life seal hung from his neck, in the middle of his chest, as if it was a cock's red wattle for all to see.

Tau glared at She-Aba. "Plain suits me fine!"

"Tau, why are you here?" Lilith asked, cutting in.

He reached inside his pouch and produced a small, round disk attached to a thin leather thong. He dangled it. "I believe this belongs to you. I tied it to this leather strip so you wouldn't lose it again."

Lilith's eyes grew big. *My life seal!* Her mind raced. She knew she had it with her when she left the market after that fiasco with Mica. She mentally retraced her steps. *No, not the oil vender, I still had it with me at the time.* Her thoughts deepened. She-Aba had met her by the fountain, and she had her life seal then because she showed it to She-Aba in a crying fit, then placed it into her satchel. Then Lilith frowned.

"It doesn't look very fashionable."

Tau jerked. "Don't you Atchas possess any manners? A thank you would be nice."

Lilith sighed. "Thank you, Tau, for returning the bane of my existence."

"Life seals are not to be taken lightly." Tau wagged a finger. "A life seal is your pledge to Ra and should be taken seriously. You must understand this!"

"Yeah, well understand this, bug-boy!" Lilith hurled one of her sandals at him. She missed, as usual. That didn't stop her. She took off her other sandal and raised it.

"Stop playing around and let me in. I need to get back to assist Mica at the Temple of Sacrifice."

Lilith froze. *Mica?* Her heart raced. Tau was with Mica. She dropped her sandal. "Um, sure, come in, Tau, the front door is open."

"What are you doing?" She-Aba asked.

"Showing Tau that I have manners." Lilith rushed out of her room.

She-Aba clicked her tongue and shouted, "You say manners. I say manure."

Ignoring She-Aba's remark, Lilith raced down the stone-cut staircase. Her bare feet slid across the marble tiles. The air seemed heavy tonight, as if she had to cut a path through it. Reaching the door, she wrenched it open, grabbed Tau by the arm, and pulled him in. He stumbled across a few tiles, then stopped and twirled around. His brown eyes were wide, his brow furrowed.

"Have you inhaled a bad batch of incense?" Tau asked.

"No. Why?"

"You've never been this eager to see me," he replied, crossing his arms over his bare chest.

"Eager to see you, no," She-Aba said, sashaying down the stairs. "But to hear what you have to say about a certain someone would be a definite yes."

Lilith blinked. She-Aba had completely changed outfits in the time she'd run down the stairs to let Tau in. Instead of wearing the blue-green sheath she arrived in, she now wore a shorter yellow and white sheath with braided straps and a pearl-embellished belt. Gold bracelets dangled from both wrists, and a mix of coral and diamond rings were set on most of her fingers. A snake-skin satchel and matching open-toed shoes completed her new look.

"How... how did you change so fast?" Lilith gawked at her.

She-Aba grinned. "You have your skills, I have mine."

"What certain someone?" Tau asked, standing in front of Lilith, his arms still crossed.

Lilith scowled at She-Aba, then looked Tau in the eye, and said, "Um, I was wondering if Mica was still—" Her mind searched for the proper words "—upset with me?"

Tau smirked. He uncrossed his arms, opened his fist, and handed Lilith her life seal.

She took it politely, still waiting on his answer.

"Aren't you going to wear it so you don't lose it again?" He sounded irritated.

Her brows arched. She swiftly guided her life seal over her head and let it drop under her gown to rest on her chest. It felt surprisingly light. "There. Satisfied?"

"Don't you want to know where I found it?" Tau asked.

No. Not really. Lilith pursed her lips. "Okay, where did I leave it?"

"It was in the fountain by the market. My younger brother, Seth, found it. I immediately knew it was yours and raced over here before you suffered the wrath of Ra."

Legend of the Timekeepers

Lilith scratched her chin. "Mmm, there must be a hole in my satchel. Surely Ra wouldn't be mad at me for that."

She-Aba gasped. "A hole in your satchel? The satchel I made for you? Not possible. I use only the finest threads to create my masterpieces! There must be some mistake."

"There are no mistakes, no accidents!" Tau shouted, his voice echoing down the hall. "You forget that you use threads Ra created. Perhaps our god is teaching you a lesson. You must learn that only Ra creates perfection, and lowly humans are here to serve."

In five long steps, She-Aba was face-to-face with Tau. Her shoes gave her some advantage, but her eyes did all the talking as they burned into his. "You forget I was born here, so don't treat me like a lowly Atch—" She stopped herself, and sheepishly glanced at Lilith. "Um, what I mean is…is—"

"No, do go on, She-Aba," Lilith cut in. She glared at her. "Explain what you mean."

"I…I didn't intend to use that word, it…it was an accident," She-Aba stammered.

"There are no accidents!" Lilith and Tau yelled in unison.

Knock, knock, knock. "Hello. Lilith? Tau?"

Lilith straightened. *Oh-my-Poseidon, That sounds like—*

"Hello, Mica," Tau answered, breaking Lilith's thoughts.

She-Aba let out her breath. "Thank you, Ra," she muttered.

"Oh, um, h-hello, Mica," Lilith replied, tripping over her words. "Won't you come in?"

There was a moment of silence. "I will if you open the door for me," he replied.

"O-Of course, sorry, silly me." Lilith reached for the door. Her legs trembled.

As soon as the door swung open, she could smell him. Fragrant sandalwood mixed with a hint of jasmine and spice. She leaned against the door, drinking him in. Mica was dressed in his initiate's pale green robe, matching pants and sash, and headband, which held his sun-hued hair perfectly in place. Like Tau, he displayed his life seal on a leather thong around his neck. His snake charmer's flute was stuffed in the side of his sash. He had a crafted leather satchel etched with a red serpent hanging over one of his shoulders and carried a large linen sack in one hand. Lilith swore she saw it move.

"May I come in, Lilith?" Mica asked cautiously.

Jolted back, she nodded. "Yes…yes of course."

Sharon Ledwith

He offered her a half-smile and walked in.

"I thought I was to meet you back at the Temple of Sacrifice?" Tau asked. "Was there success with the human-animal hybrid? Did the surgeon remove the accessory?"

She-Aba perked up. "Accessory? Did something go wrong with someone's wardrobe? I can help with that, you know."

Tau rolled his eyes. "Not that kind of accessory, *fire-head*. I'm talking about an animal accessory—a deformity, like a wing or a claw."

"A wing or a claw?" Lilith asked. "What exactly do they do in the Temple of Sacrifice?"

Tau looked at She-Aba, then back at Mica, who was scowling at him. He shrunk, then shrugged. "Don't...don't you know?"

"Know what? I thought the Temple of Sacrifice was nothing more than a place of healing. Are you telling me that it's not?"

Tau started to open his mouth. "It is," Mica said, cutting him off. "It's also a sacred place that was built to help the human-animal hybrids adapt to a more...human existence. The patient must make a sacrifice through the removal of their animal part, like Tau suggested, a wing or a claw, if they are to be accepted as humans. The process is painful and many surgeries are required, but the end result connects them back to their humanness."

"That...that sounds like torture," Lilith said, blinking.

Mica frowned. "Is it not torture to not know who you are? These poor victims are so lost in themselves that they do not know where they belong, or what their purpose is."

Lilith's shoulders slumped. What he said made sense. *But still...*

Mica cleared his throat. "There is an urgent matter that requires your father's attention. Is he available for an audience?"

"He's busy," She-Aba blurted. Then she crept closer. "He's in the presence of the Children of the Law of One." She brought a finger to her glossy lips.

"I wouldn't normally bother Segund, but Istulo sent me to deliver this to him." Mica patted the leather bag hanging over his shoulder.

Lilith reached out to grab the satchel's strap. "I'll take it to my father, Mica. I know the proper procedure to rouse him from a deep trance."

Mica snatched her hand in mid-air. Then he smiled fully. His thumb caressed the inside of her wrist. "I'm under strict orders by the high priestess herself, Lilith. Only I may hand this over to

Legend of the Timekeepers

Segund. I'm sorry, I trust you, but it would violate my vows as an initiate."

Lilith didn't hear a word Mica just said. Her whole body was singing as he continued to stroke her wrist.

"Are you okay, Lilith?" She-Aba asked. "You're turning redder than my hair."

"And that's not good in the gods' eyes," Tau added.

"Huh? Oh, um, I guess I'm still getting used to the climate here." Lilith withdrew her hand from Mica to fan her face. Then the linen bag in his hand moved.

She stepped back and pointed at the bag. "What's in there?"

Mica laughed. "My cobra. He's been restless lately, so I thought I'd ask one of the animal healers to check him over when I return to the Temple of Sacrifice."

"Maybe he ate a bad rat," Tau said, scratching his nose.

"Or maybe he listened to your flute playing too many times," Mica replied with a chuckle. He looked back at Lilith and met her eyes. "I could leave Kheti with you if you like. I will only be a moment with your father. One of the first lessons we're taught as initiates is to gently awake someone in meditation."

Lilith gulped, melting into his gaze. Her legs started to shake again.

"I'll watch Kheti, Mica." Tau held out his hand.

Mica slapped it away. "No way, you'll probably make him sick!"

"I agree. Tau makes me sick too." She-Aba broke out in laughter.

Lilith giggled, then composed herself and said, "I don't suppose it would do any harm to interrupt Father briefly. But please, remember that you'll be in the presence of the Children of the Law of One. Respect is a priority."

Mica nodded, then handed the linen sack containing Kheti to her. Lilith froze. She stared at the bag, then looked at him. "Um, no, you take that thing with you, Mica."

His fair brows rose. "You sure?"

She nodded vehemently. *Oh, yes, I'm sure.* She pointed toward the hallway past the deep purple curtains. "Father is at the end of the corridor, in the Golden Serpent room."

"I won't be long," Mica said, then winked at her. "And, just so you know, I think my life seal is dead wrong."

"Mine too!" She-Aba snapped her fingers. "See, Lilith, I told you something's not right with life seals lately."

46

Sharon Ledwith

"Well, mine's fine," Tau said indignantly, patting his life seal resting on his chest.

Mica smiled one last time before he strode down the hallway lit with crystal clusters.

Lilith watched him leave, twisting at her coiled snake bracelet. Suddenly, she felt a sharp twinge in her belly.

"Stop spraying me, She-Aba," Tau yelled.

"You want to attract a suitor, don't you, Tau? You'll never attract one smelling like that," she said, stuffing the small vial of perfume back into her bag.

"Smelling like what?" He fanned the air.

She-Aba smirked. "Beetle dung."

A crystal-shattering scream spiraled down the hallway.

"Father?" Lilith shouted. No response. "Mica?" There was still no response.

Tau darted down the hall first. "Do you two need an invitation?" he yelled over his shoulder.

Lilith followed Tau, her mind going in circles.

"Slow down, I can't run very well in these shoes," She-Aba shouted after them.

Skidding to a stop, Lilith almost banged into Tau, now stationed at the threshold of the Golden Serpent room. Her mouth fell open. Mica was gone, disappeared. His cobra, Kheti, was loose. It hovered over her father, who had collapsed on the smooth, shiny floor behind his meditation pillow. She could make out two small red streams running down the back of his hand. The seventh Arch of Atlantis hummed a queasy vibration, as if something had disturbed its frequency.

Lilith glanced up at the arch, and her eyes widened. The crystal trident her father used to activate the link between the Children of the Law of One and himself had vanished from the keystone of the arch. The etched trident outline the length of her hand now lay barren and empty, as if it had lost its soul mate. Streams of golden light haphazardly shot out of the archway, creating a chaotic cosmic light show.

Her stomach twisted as if one hundred baby snakes had hatched inside it. Cobra venom was more powerful than a white crawler's poison. She knew that, and by the look of Tau's ashen face, he knew that too. Her father lay dying before her. Mica was nowhere to be

47

Legend of the Timekeepers

seen. And the thing she dreaded the most was only five strides away.

She-Aba shrieked, making Lilith and Tau jump.

The cobra turned and hissed. It made itself taller, flared out its hood, and started to advance on Lilith, Tau, and She-Aba where they stood in the doorway.

5. Time Flows Through Us

"**M**ove out of the way, I've got this," She-Aba said, pulling off her satchel. She started swinging it.

"What are you doing, fire-head!" Tau screamed. "That…that's a cobra!"

"You see a snake. I see a new pair of shoes," she replied.

The cobra reared then struck, but not before She-Aba whacked it across the head, sending the snake flying across the floor.

Lilith saw her opportunity and sprinted to her father's side. She kneeled and put her ear to his heart. *Still beating, thank Poseidon.* She grabbed the wide meditation pillow and shoved it under her father's head. The record keeper lying on the pillow was flung across the floor and landed in front of the glowing archway. Then she looked around for something to wrap around his hand to cut off the poison coursing through his body. She felt his body jerk and, out of the corner of her eye, saw the belt She-Aba had dressed him with being yanked away. Fighting tears, Lilith looked up.

Tau now had the belt in his hands. He wrapped one end around his hand, turned, and whistled at the dazed cobra. "Sorry, Kheti, you leave me no choice."

Legend of the Timekeepers

Tau stepped forward and cracked the belt like a whip. But instead of hitting the cobra in the head, it returned with a smack to his nose. Blood spurted everywhere. Tau released the belt, took a few strides back until he smacked into the arch, and crumbled to the floor. He cupped his nose.

She-Aba clicked her tongue. "If you want a job done right, give it to a girl."

She lunged for the belt and lashed out at the cobra, using the heavier end as leverage. One of the spiked metal disks struck the snake's right eye. The serpent hissed before hitting the floor. She-Aba didn't give it time to recover. She rushed over and, with the heel of her shoe, crushed the cobra's skull. Its tail gyrated until there was no life left and went limp.

The Arch of Atlantis ceased showering the room with its golden lights and began to draw the light back through the archway. The humming dropped in resonance to a sickly sound, as if something inside of it was preparing to die.

"What has happened?" an old voice wheezed from the doorway.

"Istulo!" Lilith shouted. "Please, come and heal my father! He's been bitten by Mica's cobra!"

The high priestess gasped. She ambled over as fast as she could, trying not to get her feet caught up in her white robe, and bent down over Segund. Lilith heard her knees crackle like dry papyrus. Istulo glanced at Tau slouched on the floor coddling his face. "Is he bitten as well?"

"Tau will be fine." She-Aba crouched next to Lilith. "Unless you think belts are poisonous."

Istulo frowned, then examined Segund's hand. She grunted. "I trusted Mica. I see the gods have tested me, and I have failed."

"Why would Mica do this?" Lilith asked, aware of sharp pains in her throat.

"He seeks revenge," Istulo replied. "His heart is still in darkness."

"Revenge?" Tau said through his hands, sounding muffled. "On whom?"

"On those of his past, and of Atlantis's past. He hates the Sons of Belial, who killed his parents, and will do whatever it takes to change his future."

50

Before Lilith could ask what she meant, Istulo wheezed and said, "This is bad. She-Aba, go get me a bowl of water, some linens, and the dead cobra."

She-Aba arched her perfectly plucked red brows. "The dead cobra?"

"I need to mix a potion using the cobra's sacrifice. Pray Ra has seen to it that I have what I need in my pouch."

Tears now streamed down Lilith's face. "I…I will."

"Me too, we're in this together." She-Aba squeezed Lilith's shoulder before she left to do Istulo's bidding.

Tau groaned. "I don't care what She-Aba says, that belt bit me. Hey, what is this?" He pointed at a small book on the tile in front of him.

Lilith took her eyes off her father for a moment. "Father's record keeper. He uses it to scribe the messages from the Children of the Law of One."

"Your father is a scribe?" Tau asked, wiping blood from his nose. He reached for the record keeper.

"He's a lot of things, Tau. Right now, he's just my father."

Istulo started to chant. She retrieved a small, crystal mortar from her pouch, opened the dead cobra's jaws, and squeezed the inside of its mouth near the fangs. Droplets of a yellow liquid dripped into the mortar. Continuing to chant, her gravelly voice grated against Lilith's ears, and Lilith winced. She didn't know what was worse—Istulo's chanting or the Arch of Atlantis's discordant droning. Loud, scraping footsteps announced She-Aba's return. Her snakeskin satchel was back over one shoulder while the other shoulder was draped in white linens. In both hands, she carried a large ceramic bowl.

"Here." She placed the bowl down by Istulo.

Segund roused. "L-Lilith," he muttered.

"I'm here, Father. So is Istulo. She'll heal you. Stay with me."

His mouth opened like a naked baby bird. "M-Mica w-went th-through arch wh-while it w-was o-opened t-to our p-past. H-He t-took t-the tri-dent. Need…it."

"Never mind Mica, Father, you need me."

"N-No. T-T-Time f-flows—" he attempted to point at Lilith, then dropped his hand "—th-through…us. Through…you. K-Keep t-time s-safe. F-Find M-Mica. B-Bring him home."

Legend of the Timekeepers

"What's your father saying, Lilith?" She-Aba asked, ripping strips of linen for Istulo. She dipped one strip into the water, rolled it up, and placed it on Segund's beading forehead.

"I'm not sure. Time flows through us. Through me. Keep time safe. He wants me to find Mica and bring him home. It doesn't make any sense." Lilith stroked her father's soft beard.

Then, as if given an awakening jolt, the Arch of Atlantis started to hum louder, outdoing Istulo's chants. A beam of golden light, appearing in the form of a serpent's head, shot out of the archway. It surrounded Tau, who was kneeling with his head down, looking into the open record keeper. Stunned, he let out a visceral gasp, like his insides were being torn out. His brown eyes grew big, and as if being commanded by the serpent light, he pulled a long, thin piece of crystal out of the spine of the record keeper and started to scribe inside it.

Istulo continued to chant, choosing to focus on healing Segund. Lilith was torn between the two spectacles manifesting before her— Tau, enwrapped in a golden serpent-like light, and Istulo, still squeezing liquid from the lifeless cobra. Then, as if on cue, Istulo dropped the cobra, added a dash of white powder to the liquid in the mortar, and spooned in a small amount of water from the bowl with her cupped palm.

Suddenly, Tau was released from the serpent light. He fell forward before catching himself. Shaken, he stood up, wobbled, and glanced into the record keeper.

"Tau? Are you hurt?" Lilith asked.

He shook his head. "I'm fine. But it seems I've scribed into your father's record keeper, and I don't remember doing it."

"What's it say, Tau?" She-Aba asked, standing. She moved to peer over his shoulder. "Hmm, looks like a jumble of beetle footprints to me."

Tau scowled. "That's because girls don't know how to scribe properly."

"Hold your father's head up for me, Lilith," Istulo said, her voice sounding hoarse.

Propping up Segund's head, Lilith kept it still while Istulo poured the mixture of cobra's liquid, white powder, and water down his throat.

"What did you take from the snake's mouth?" Lilith asked as Istulo wiped a running drop away from his chin.

52

Sharon Ledwith

"Poison," she replied with no emotion.

Lilith balked. "You...you made him drink the cobra's poison? But...but that's already in his body!"

Istulo put her hand up. "In alchemy, you fight fire with fire, Lilith. I know what I am doing. I am trained in the art of potions. You need to learn to trust. All we can do now is wait. Segund is in Ra's hands." Then she clapped three times over Lilith's barely breathing father and went into a trance.

Wiping her eyes, Lilith bent down to kiss her father's forehead. The heat and stickiness melded with her lips and tasted like melted salt. Lilith fixed his shirt, slowly stood, and walked over to Tau and She-Aba. The Arch of Atlantis still hummed steadily, the sound starting to make her feel woozy. *Why did Mica do this?* Her fingers curled into her palms, and she sucked in her stomach.

She-Aba reached out to hug her. "It will be all right, Lilith. Istulo will heal your father."

Lilith unfurled her fingers and hugged She-Aba back. She squeezed her eyes shut to wring out her tears, then opened them. She wanted to melt into the deep bronze color of the room, find comfort from one of the four huge tapestries hanging against each wall, but Tau obscured her view.

Tau looked up from the record keeper. The sides of his eyes crinkled as he caught Lilith staring at him. "Don't expect me to give you a hug, Atcha-girl," he said with a slight grin. Lilith reached out to snatch the record keeper away from him. "Hey, I wasn't finished reading that!"

"Is that what you were doing?" She-Aba let Lilith go. "It looked more like you were trying to understand what you scribed."

Tau sighed. "I...I was. I don't know the meaning of some of the words."

Lilith looked over the papyrus pages. "Is this a riddle or a poem you wrote, Tau?"

"What's a riddle?" She-Aba asked.

"What's a poem?" Tau asked.

Lilith rolled her eyes. "Nevermind. Just listen, and we'll try to figure out what this means—*Greedy and wicked these people have become, ignoring to follow the Law of One. Return to the City of the Golden Gates, the One who must banish evil, by the end of the first major quake.*"

Tau shrugged. "Where's the City of the Golden Gates?"

53

Legend of the Timekeepers

"Yeah, and who are the greedy and wicked people?" She-Aba asked.

The Arch of Atlantis's humming instantly changed from a low drone into a high piercing pitch. Three golden beams of light snaked out of the archway, and instead of transforming into serpents, the tri-lights burst into a vibrant spiraling rainbow and pulled Lilith, She-Aba, and Tau into the archway.

Lilith clasped the record keeper close to her heart, fearing if she didn't, she may lose it forever. They were falling, whirling around in mid-air like drops of rain in the wind. A sense of calm, of peace, entered her mind, extinguishing her fear in that moment. The whirling rainbow was pulling her, She-Aba, and Tau somewhere, and at the same time it was ensuring her in its own way that all was well. A feeling of floating, of being light as a feather, brushed her insides, making her skin ripple. Curious, Lilith held one arm out, keeping her other hand securely over the record keeper. She tried to catch the air, slow herself down, as the spiral drew them deeper and deeper inside, as if they were being swallowed by a huge serpent.

She-Aba clenched her knees together while trying to hold her sheath and satchel down. "My clothes will be ruined if we don't slow down!" she shrieked.

"It's always about you, isn't it, fire-head?" Tau said. Then he spread out his arms and legs. "Ohhh, this is how a hawk must feel when it soars!"

She-Aba grabbed Tau's ankle with her free hand and gave him a spin. "And this…is what a flailing scarab feels like, bug-boy!"

"That's not funny, fire-head!" Tau yelled, wobbling around.

"It is from this angle," She-Aba replied, giggling.

Lilith's stomach felt as if it were almost stuck in her throat. Shifting her body in flight, she maneuvered over to She-Aba and Tau. "Did the golden serpent light say anything to you while it was wrapped around you, Tau?"

Before he had a chance to answer, Lilith felt her body slow down, as if a sudden wind had pushed her back up, then gently lowered her down. Gaining her balance, she felt the spongy ground underneath her bare feet. She-Aba's landing was not so graceful, as she stumbled on her high heels and fell into a wide-leafed plant with pink flowers. Tau never made it to the ground. Caught in between two thick branches of a tree that looked as if it had been planted upside-down, he hung, chasing the air with his legs and going

54

Sharon Ledwith

nowhere. As their surroundings became clearer, Lilith noticed that they had been dumped in the middle of what looked like a tropical forest. It was a refreshing change from the Black Land's barren landscape, but it was unfamiliar.

"W-Where are we?" She-Aba asked, crawling out of the plant.

"I-I'm not sure," Lilith replied. Her nose flared. The air smelled fresh, almost pure to her.

"Well, we're not in the desert anymore," Tau said, wiggling and huffing. "Could you two get me down?"

She-Aba smirked. "What's the magic word?"

Tau stopped squirming between the branches. "Huh? Magic word? How would I know, I'm not a magus!"

"You're not very bright, either," She-Aba replied. "What word do you use when you want something?"

Tau snorted. "Now!"

Lilith rolled her eyes. She passed the record keeper to She-Aba, then stuck her foot into the closest, deepest crevice in the tree. She pulled herself up, found another crevice, and pulled herself up again. She looked back down at She-Aba. "Go cut a vine for Tau to use to climb down."

"What's a vine?" She-Aba asked, frowning.

Lilith sighed. "Over there, hanging from that tree. It looks like a rope. Haven't you ever seen one?"

"No. I live in a desert. In fact, I find it quite warm and damp here. Not the best place for my hair."

"There is no place for your hair, fire-head," Tau said indignantly.

She-Aba grunted. She opened her satchel, slid the record keeper in, and pulled out the metal clipper she used to cut and style hair. Lilith hid an emerging smile as she observed her friend. Walking proved to be anything but easy for She-Aba, as the forest floor appeared to want to swallow her shoes. Reaching for a long strong vine that crept around the base of a tree as if it were a snake, She-Aba sliced through it with ease, untangled it, and hobbled back to Lilith and Tau.

A rancorous scream permeated through the forest. She-Aba froze in her tracks, the vine she cut hanging lifeless in her hand. "W-What was that?"

Lilith's whole body prickled. *No, it can't be, can it? That would be impossible.*

55

Legend of the Timekeepers

She turned to scan the area. Tau wouldn't quit wiggling. She reached for his arm and squeezed. "Stop that, I'm trying to—"

Another scream, this time closer, rolled out through the leaves.

"Oh, Poseidon, it is," Lilith said, feeling her heart start to race. "Quick, She-Aba, throw up the vine and go hide! Now!"

"What's going on, Lilith?" Tau asked. "Why do you sound so frightened?"

Lilith looked around again. "Because a wyvern is hunting us."

"A…what?" She-Aba asked.

"A wyvern. It looks like a huge snake with wings, feet like a hawk's, and a tail like a white crawler."

She-Aba huffed. "Excuse, me, Miss Bossy, but I think I proved that I can handle a snake just fine."

"For once would you just do as you're told, fire-head," Tau said. "Throw up the vine!"

"You mean this vine, Tau?" She-Aba swung it in her hand.

"She-Aba, you don't understand, wyverns aren't like cobras," Lilith explained. "You've never seen one before, so you have no idea what they're capable of."

"So enlighten me, then. How do you know so much about these snake-like creatures?"

Lilith scanned the area one more time before she said, "They're native to only one place on earth."

"And where's that?" Tau asked, grunting as he gripped the tree branch.

Lilith licked her dry lips and said, "Atlantis."

56

Sharon Ledwith

6. The First Timekeepers

"**D**id...did you just say Atlantis? Atlantis, as in your home country?" She-Aba asked.

"Atlantis as in your now sunken country?" Tau asked.

Lilith nodded. "I know it makes no sense, but wyverns were only bred on Atlantis to protect our coastline."

Another shriek permeated Lilith's ears. She balked. "She-Aba—the vine!"

She-Aba pitched the vine, not realizing that its end was tangled around her feet. As Lilith and Tau yanked up on it, She-Aba fell backwards. "Stop pulling, I'm caught!"

"Well, get uncaught, fire-head, we need the vine!" Tau shouted down.

Hearing branches snap and crack, Lilith and Tau turned their heads. They dropped their jaws, and the vine, at the same time. A wyvern broke into the clearing—a young one—Lilith guessed, judging by its size, as it was no bigger than a full-grown horse. Its translucent wings flapped, its green, leathery skin rippled, and it opened its reptilian jaws. A long, forked tongue slithered out, as if tasting their smell, drinking in the perfume of their sweat. Strutting like a cock ready to do battle, it whipped its long tail side to side,

57

Legend of the Timekeepers

showing off its poisonous barb as if it were an ornament to be revered. The wyvern's nostrils flared once, twice, three times before it let out another shriek from his monstrous mouth and charged them.

"Oh-my-Poseidon! Run, She-Aba!" Lilith screamed, trying to break a branch off the tree.

"I-I-I'm trying!" She-Aba yelled, still struggling with the vine.

A roar sounded from behind the advancing wyvern. Lilith had managed to snap off a branch and pitch it at the winged serpent. Her aim was dead on, whacking it on the head. It stopped, shook its head and neck, making the wormy beard on its chin wiggle, and glared at Lilith. It let out a shriek that made her insides shrink. The wyvern flapped its wings, preparing for attack, but was clawed in the face by what appeared to be a human-animal hybrid half its size.

The hybrid stood upright, roared, grabbed one of the wyvern's wings, and tugged it toward its back. Losing its footing, the wyvern shrieked, gnashed its jaws from side-to-side, and flailed its barbed tail around the air in an attempt to swat the hybrid. The wyvern's attacker pulled the wing harder until it was dragged down to the ground.

"Watch the tail!" Lilith yelled.

The hybrid looked up in time to avoid the tail. Although he looked and dressed like a man, he possessed the claws and tail of a lion. He glanced at Lilith for a moment. Olive eyes bored into her. His nose was long, his cheekbones high. He had a shaggy black mane for hair and a long, braided goatee. He was wearing a burgundy tunic with the insignia of a golden serpent wrapped around his left arm. This marked him a guardian of the Temple of the Sun—a common purpose for human-lion hybrids.

"Etan!" a voice yelled from the forest.

"Who said that?" Tau asked, still struggling between the branches.

"There—" Lilith pointed. "—running out from behind those sprawling shrubs. A boy about your age."

"Not a boy, a…a *man*." She-Aba finally freed herself. She ran her fingers through her hair. "And he's a fine-looking specimen from what I see."

"Stay where you are! I swore to your father to keep you safe!" the human-lion hybrid named Etan growled back to the new-comer as he pinned the wyvern down harder.

58

Sharon Ledwith

"For Ra's sake, throw up the vine, fire-head, my legs are cramping!" Tau yelled.

Lilith caught the vine, wrapped it around the branches Tau was pinned between, then reached over, grabbed one of his feet, and guided his foot toward a notch in the tree. "Push hard, Tau, set yourself free!"

Tau grunted as if he were giving birth and pushed himself up and out. He grasped the vine and climbed down with ease, mimicking a monkey. Then Lilith reached for the vine, swung off the rough tree trunk, and started to slide down just as the wyvern let out an angry, piercing shriek. Startled, she jerked and the vine snapped. She-Aba broke her fall.

"Ohhh!" She-Aba screamed, almost matching the wyvern's horrible wail. "My foot!"

"Ohhh, my ears," Tau muttered, covering his ears.

Lilith heard the sound of hurried footsteps crunch through the spongy ground to beat a path toward them.

"Are you hurt?" someone with a distinct Atlantean accent asked.

Lilith looked up. The young man who had run out of the forest hovered above her and She-Aba. He had curly, sandy hair which stuck out every which way, and soft brown eyes. He was dressed in a linen tunic and pants, with a purple sash and palm leaf sandals. Despite his plain clothing, everything about his manner and stance told Lilith that he came from a house of privilege. He leaned against his staff, as if he had nothing better to do.

She cleared her throat. "Um, I wouldn't worry too much about us, seeing as your—"

"It's…it's broken!" She-Aba cut her off.

"Your foot is broken?" Tau asked in a concerned tone.

She-Aba sniffed. "No, my heel! Now my shoe is ruined!"

Lilith rolled her eyes. She got up, brushed herself off, looked at the young man hovering over her friend, and said, "She's all yours."

Etan ripped out a painful roar. Lilith whirled around. The wyvern had managed to dig one of its sharp talons into his leg. His grip was starting to weaken. The wyvern's tail swung around enough for Lilith to see a small tattoo above the barbed tail. Her eyes widened. Uncle Kukulkan had once told her that to ensure their safety wyvern breeders implanted a small poisonous sac inside the tails of young wyverns, and marked the area with a tattoo. If a wyvern suddenly became unruly, then the breeder smashed a rod against the tattoo to

59

Legend of the Timekeepers

release the poison into the wyvern's body, killing it instantly. Panicking, Lilith looked around for a makeshift weapon. The only possible weapon was being used as a post. She didn't hesitate and grabbed the staff the stranger was leaning on.

"Tau, pick up the vine and follow me!" Lilith yelled.

"Huh? Why?" Tau asked.

"You're a farmer's son. Surely you know how to rope a goat," she answered.

"Goats, yes. That—" Tau pointed, while gathering the vine "—not so much."

"All you need to do is rope its tail. I'll do the rest with this staff."

Tau groaned as he made a loop with the vine. "Atchas make no sense."

Lilith frowned. "What do you mean?"

"You're afraid of cobras, but not afraid of those things?"

The wyvern shrieked as it thrashed its head and long neck.

"Come on, Tau, the hybrid is losing his grip!"

Lilith sprinted and circled the wyvern on one side, while Tau ran toward the opposite side and waved the noose over his head. With his tongue sticking out the side of his mouth, Tau threw the vine and caught the tip of its barbed tail. Threading the vine around his torso, he yanked on the tail. The wyvern screeched, swung its head in Tau's direction, and snapped its jaws, just missing his foot.

"Hurry, Lilith, before this oversized lizard reaches me!"

Lilith targeted the dark tattoo shaped like two connected circles above the barb, raised the staff and swung it with enough force to hit the tattoo dead-on. The wyvern jumped at the blow. Hissing and wailing, it started to convulse and drool as the poison from the implanted sac swiftly shot through its body. Etan released his hold, flicked his tail, and motioned for Lilith and Tau to move away. The wyvern, now free, thrashed and railed for three more breaths before it fell deadly still.

"Quick thinking, Lilith," Tau said as he joined her. "How did you know what to do?"

"Simple. We needed to fight fire with fire, like Istulo did with my father," she replied. "I knew that under the tattoo above the wyvern's barbed tail was a poisonous sac placed there by its breeder, so I thought if we could get close enough to break the sac then—"

60

"—it would poison itself," Tau cut in, finishing for her. "Good call, Atcha-girl."

"Thank you," the human-lion hybrid said, bowing. His voice sounded beastly, deep.

Lilith squeezed the staff. "We should be the ones thanking you. If it wasn't for you, my friends and I would be wyvern-fodder by now."

"Unless it got to She-Aba first," Tau added with a grin. "She would have left a bad taste in its mouth, and it would have left us alone."

Lilith burst out laughing.

"Did I miss a joke?" She-Aba asked, hobbling on one foot while the young man had his arm wrapped around her waist.

"Oh, there's always something to laugh about when you're around, fire-head."

She-Aba huffed. "If you don't show some proper manners, I won't introduce you to my new friend."

"Poor friend," Tau muttered.

Etan hid a smile. Lilith did too, then said, "I'm Lilith, and this is Tau. I see She-Aba has already presented herself."

The young man bowed. "My name is Ajax-ol. And this—" he waved a hand toward the hybrid "—is Etan, my guardian."

"Your guardian? I thought Etan was a guardian of the Temple of the Sun?" Lilith looked at him. "He wears the insignia on his left arm."

Suddenly, a tremor rose up through the ground. She-Aba almost fell again, but Ajax-ol held her tight. She made a cooing sound and snuggled to him.

"I am," Etan answered, as the tremor passed. "I also serve the House of Ajxor."

"The House of Ajxor? As in Admiral Ajxor?" Lilith asked.

"My father is not an admiral," Ajax-ol replied, tipping his head slightly. "At least not yet. Unless—" he looked at her squarely "—you know something I don't?"

Lilith frowned. "No. I thought the history scrolls state—" She stopped herself. Her skin prickled. *This must be Atlantis as it was a hundred years ago, before the first major earthquake. This is what Father was scribing about in his record keeper when Mica interrupted him.* her eyes widened. *Mica must be here too!* The ground rumbled and shook again.

Legend of the Timekeepers

Lilith fell forward and Etan grabbed her arms. She winced, feeling the power of his grip.

"My apologies," he said. "Did I hurt you?"

She shook her head. "I'm fine, just a little confused. Can you tell me who is in power?"

"Some say King Elem is, but I say Belial holds the real power," Etan growled as he released Lilith.

"Who is Belial?" Tau asked.

Etan's whole face drew in, as a wary, low growl developed in the back of his throat, and he swished his tail. "Where are you from? You talk with a strange dialect."

"Both She-Aba and Tau are from the Black Land," Lilith replied quickly before Tau answered. "I used to, um, I mean I dwell in the City of the Golden Gates, in the advisor's section."

Ajax-ol jerked. He slipped his arm away from She-Aba, who stumbled back. "These two are from the Black Land? I've heard only savages dwell there."

"Savages?" Tau said indignantly. "You have some nerve, Atcha—"

Lilith didn't give Tau a chance to finish. She clipped him across the back of the head. "Silence! You must never address anyone from the House of Ajxor in that manner. You're here to serve my family, and you need to learn respect for our people!"

Tau's eyes bugged. He rubbed the back of his head. Then Lilith looked at She-Aba, who was having difficulty balancing on one shoe. "And you—" she pointed at She-Aba "—take that shoe off and walk with dignity. You'll never be groomed as an Atlantean's servant if you are not appropriately dressed."

"S-S-Servant?" She-Aba stammered.

Lilith clapped her hands three times. "Are you both forgetting how much trouble it was for my family to have you shipped here? The travel costs alone made us...*spiral*."

She-Aba's eyes widened. So did Tau's. They glanced at each other and nodded.

Lilith inhaled sharply. *Good. We're all on the same scroll now.* She handed Ajax-ol his staff back and said, "Thank you for the use of your staff, Ajax-ol."

He grabbed her left hand in mid-air and inspected the orichalcum snake bracelet her Uncle Kukulkan had given her before they left

62

Atlantis. "Etan, look, she wears the talisman from the House of Seers."

Lilith thought she heard Etan purr. "Yes, it appears so, Ajax-ol. Lilith must be in exile as well," he said.

"House of Seers? Exile? What does that mean?" She-Aba asked.

"In my house, a servant does not speak until spoken to," Ajax-ol said sternly.

"It's all right, Ajax-ol," Lilith said, patting his hand. "In our house, we teach our servants to ask questions if they don't understand. My father says it breaks down barriers and builds better relations."

Ajax-ol laughed. "Belial would do well to listen to your father."

"Belial listens to no one, Ajax-ol, that is why your father had me take you here," Etan added.

"Yes, Lilith's father had me take Lilith and her woman-servant here too." Tau puffed out his chest. "I even had to face a cobra to carry out my duty."

"Excuse me, bug-boy?" She-Aba blurted. "Who faced the cobra?"

Lilith waved them off. "Why were you exiled, Ajax-ol?"

He looked at Lilith warily. "Why were *you* exiled?"

She felt her heart skip a beat. "Oh, well, you see, it's complicated really—"

"She trusted the wrong person," Tau replied, cutting in.

Ajax-ol laughed. "You too?"

Lilith's shoulders sagged. "Yes. His name is Mica."

"Her name is Zurumu," he said, shrugging. "I should have known better. She has bright red hair like your woman-servant."

Tau guffawed.

She-Aba's face turned as red the setting sun.

"Most of the high priestesses have red hair, Ajax-ol," Etan added. "You happened to pick the wrong one to put your trust in."

"Really? Your high priestesses have red hair?" She-Aba asked, beaming.

"He said most, not all, fire-head," Tau said, smirking.

She-Aba opened her mouth to say something, then stopped. She pointed at Etan's leg. "Your injured leg needs attention." Then she snapped her fingers and fished around in her satchel.

Legend of the Timekeepers

Lilith glanced at Etan's leg. The bloody, torn flesh was seeping yellow liquid. She-Aba was right. The wound was starting to fester already.

"I got this at the market today. Normally, I make it into a salve to spread over my face to draw out the impurities—"

"You wasted your coins. It's not working," Tau cut in, slapping his thigh.

She-Aba rolled her eyes. "But it can also be used to heal and clean wounds, if you'll allow me."

Etan's wide nostrils flared, as if testing its fragrance. "Very well, but hurry, we need to seek shelter soon. The razor-tooth cats will be on the prowl by dusk."

She-Aba shuddered. "I don't know what you're talking about, but you don't have to tell me twice."

Another tremor rumbled through Lilith, this time throwing her to the ground. Tau was knocked over too. She sighed. She'd forgotten how unstable her homeland had been. Feeling Etan's claws wrap around her small wrists, he gently pulled her up. "The quakes are getting frequent," he said. "I fear it will get worse, before it gets better."

Lilith stared at her feet. "Trust me, it won't get any better."

"Nonsense," Ajax-ol said as he leaned on his staff and waved a hand frivolously. "Atlantis will always conquer whatever the gods will deliver. We are invincible."

Like the tremor that had just erupted through her, Lilith balled her fists, sidestepped Etan, and kicked Ajax-ol's staff out from under him. *Whump!* He fell flat on his back. She placed a foot on his chest and glared at him. "How arrogant are you to think that way! Don't you see what's happening to our land? What Belial is doing to us by abusing the power of the crystals? We're killing ourselves by killing this place!"

During Lilith's rant, her life seal attached to the thong Tau made popped out from under her gown. Etan's eyes grew large. He roared, making Lilith jump away from Ajax-ol.

Etan bent down on one knee, bowed his shaggy head, and said, "Welcome, Timekeeper. We have been waiting a long time for your arrival."

7. A Light in the Darkness

Even sitting in the brilliance of the secluded crystal cave Etan had led them to, Lilith was still in shock. *Timekeeper?* How did he know about her lifetime occupation? Better still, how did this hybrid, whom she'd never met, know what a Timekeeper was? Her father's words streamed through her like rushing water. *Time flows through us. Through you. Keep time safe. Find Mica. Bring him home.* Her shoulders slumped, her eyes welled. So far, there had been no sign of Mica. Lilith sighed. She didn't even know if her father was still alive.

"What is the House of Seers?" She-Aba whispered, warming her hands over a glowing orange crystal. "I have never heard of such a tradition in the Black Land."

Tau snorted. "Girls know nothing. The Priestesses of Ra who dwell in the Temple Beautiful are seers. To be a seer in the Black Land is to know everything."

Lilith wiped her eyes. "Not in Atlantis. To be a seer, a true seer, is to quiet the mind enough to let the silent knowledge in."

"She-Aba would not do well in that occupation." Tau chuckled.

"No, that's not what I mean," Lilith replied, toying with her snake bracelet. "My Aunt Ambeno was a seer. She told me that to

65

Legend of the Timekeepers

see things is not the same as to know things. Knowledge comes through you, not from you."

Tau frowned. He scratched his nose. "How is this possible?"

"Boys know nothing," She-Aba said, poking Tau in the ribs. "Things are what they are. Until they're not."

"What's that supposed to mean, fire-head?" Tau asked, rubbing his side.

"It means—" Ajax-ol said, sitting down next to Lilith with an armful of long, yellow fruit, "—that we all look at the world through our own eyes, and see what we want to see, until you change your view." He passed a piece of long, yellow fruit to each of them.

"Mmmm, I'm hungry," Tau said, biting into the fruit. He made a face. "Ugh! This tastes like rubbery goat dung!"

"And how do you know what that tastes like?" Lilith asked, grimacing.

He smirked. "She-Aba told me."

Lilith rolled her eyes. She grabbed the piece of fruit out of Tau's hands. "You have to peel it. See?" She pulled back the thick skin to reveal the creamy-colored fruit.

Tau stuffed it in his mouth. His eyes lit up. "Mmm, thiiss isth deliciousth!"

Ajax-ol shook his head. "Your servants don't get out much, do they?"

"Not these ones," Lilith replied, peeling a piece of fruit for herself.

"We are secure for tonight," Etan announced, returning to the crystal cave. He flicked his long tail to one side, sat on a large, flat crystal behind them, and rubbed his injured leg which was bound in palm leaves.

She-Aba handed a piece of fruit to Etan. "Here, Etan, you'll need food to help your leg heal."

Etan's nose twitched. His face wrinkled as if he were really asked to eat goat dung. "No, thank you." He unwrapped a wide leaf with one claw, picked up a chunk of bloody meat, and devoured it before Lilith had finished peeling her fruit.

She-Aba retched. She held up a finger. "One, I'm not going to ask you where that came from." Then she held up a second finger. "And two, I don't feel so hungry anymore."

"Good," Tau said, as he snatched the fruit out of her hands.

Lilith set her fruit aside, then clasped her hands. "Etan, why did you call me a Timekeeper?"

"And why have you been waiting for her?" She-Aba added.

Wiping blood away from his broad lips, Etan flicked his tongue to clean one of his large, white fangs. He stroked his braided goatee with a paw, then smiled his knowing smile. "Your medallion possesses the spiral insignia I've seen scribed on the walls of the Temple of the Sun. It has been foretold by the seers that the bearer of this insignia—a Timekeeper—will come here to bring balance and keep time flowing as it should be. You are who you are. Isn't that enough?"

No. No, it's not. Before Lilith could say a word, She-Aba squealed. "Ohh, please tell me who I am," she asked handing him her round life seal.

Etan studied it. His nostrils flared. "You share the same path with Lilith, yet you have a different purpose. I see concealment, hiding things."

She-Aba's shoulders sagged. "So much for my dreams."

"Dreams are always linked to your purpose," Etan said, passing back her life seal. "You must be patient, wait for your thoughts to clear."

"We'll be waiting a long time for that," Tau blurted.

"How does someone from the House of Seers not know her purpose?" Ajax-ol asked, popping the last bit of fruit into his mouth.

"I'm not a seer, my aunt was," Lilith said, squeezing her hands harder. She looked up at Etan. "Tell me, Etan, how does one keep time? That seems an impossible task."

Etan began rubbing his huge paws back and forth, back and forth. Then he stopped and brought them out and in, farther apart then closer together. "Do what I do. Feel the flow as you bring your hands closer together and farther away. It is nothing, yet it is everything. This is time. You cannot see it, but you can feel it push and pass through you."

Lilith copied Etan, vigorously rubbing her hands, then moving them in and out. Her hands tingled as she drew them closer then pushed away. Strange, she could feel something there between her palms, but didn't know what to do with it. She stopped, grasped her hands again, and shrugged. "If that is what you call time, then what do I do with it? I still can't keep it."

Legend of the Timekeepers

"Ultimately, the answer—" Etan pointed a sharp claw at Lilith "—lies within you, waiting to be found."

Lilith unclasped her hands and waved them in the air. "Stop with riddles!"

"Oh, Etan's very good at riddles and puzzles, Lilith," Ajax-ol said, tossing the peel of his fruit aside. "I believe it's his way of torturing us poor humans."

Lilith sat still. *Good at riddles?* She lunged for She-Aba's satchel and pulled out her father's record keeper. Scanning the pages until she found Tau's entry, she passed it to Etan. "Prove you're good and solve this riddle."

Etan's mane bristled. His paws engulfed the record keeper, and he buried his olive eyes in it. "I...don't know."

Lilith frowned. "But, I thought you were good at riddles?"

"Only when I can understand what is written, Lilith. This is not legible."

Tau, who was still stuffing his face with the yellow fruit, stopped. His cheeks were popped out, food dribbled out of his mouth. He tried to speak but gagged instead.

She-Aba giggled. "I'm getting to like this fruit more and more."

"It's the language of the Black Land's people, Etan, you're probably not familiar with it. Allow me," Lilith said, taking the record keeper from Etan. "*Greedy and wicked these people have become, ignoring to follow the Law of One. Return to the City of the Golden Gates, the One who must banish evil, by the end of the first major quake.*"

Tau finally spit out the remnants in his mouth. "How hard is it to understand our language?"

Lilith eyed him. "You were the first to make fun of how I pronounced some of your words. What do you think?"

Tau looked away sheepishly. She-Aba laughed. "I believe you have just been squashed, bug-boy."

"So what do you make of the riddle, Etan?" Ajax-ol asked, wiping his hands across his linen tunic.

Etan stroked his goatee. "It is not clear yet. I understand the first part, about how Atlanteans are moving away from their true nature by shunning the teachings of the Law of One to follow Belial's immoral path. But, the second part is veiled."

The ground shook with angered fervor. Some crystals hanging above broke apart and spiraled to the floor, splintering on impact.

68

The walls cracked, creating a fissure that looked like a slithering snake. Lilith swallowed hard. The same terrible emotions she had had before her world was torn apart surged through her body. She hugged herself just as the earth quit its rumblings.

Lilith's skin prickled, her mind cleared. *The riddle is a task given by the Children of the Law of One.* Her eyes widened.

"We need to get to the City of the Golden Gates," she said, feeling her heart grow warm. "That's what the riddle in the record keeper suggests, so that's where we're going. Maybe Mica had planned this all along, maybe that's why we're here, to bring him back with us."

"I agree. Anywhere is better than here," She-Aba said, surveying the cave's ceiling.

Ajax-ol guffawed. "Get into the City of the Golden Gates? I thought you were in exile? You'll never make it past the guards."

"Actually…I was exiled from the Black Land, not Atlantis."

Ajax-ol frowned. "I thought you said you dwelled in the City of the Golden Gates? And how does anyone get exiled from the Black Land? Usually one is exiled *to* the Black Land."

Lilith sighed. "My family used to dwell in the City of the Golden Gates. We moved to the Black Land out of…necessity."

Tau grunted. "For Ra's sake, Lilith, tell him the truth. Tell him the Children of the Law of One pulled us through the arch!"

Etan jerked. "Arch! What arch?"

"The seventh Arch of Atlantis," She-Aba said. "What arch do you think she's talking about?"

Etan's eyes became slits as he crept toward She-Aba. "Liar! All seven Arches of Atlantis are kept inside the Temple of Poseidon!" He roared. "It is only the Keeper of the Arches who is allowed to contact the Children of the Law of One!"

If Tau hadn't already made things messy enough for them, then She-Aba's comment threw muck in their faces. Lilith tossed the record keeper to Tau, then jumped in front of She-Aba and held out her hands. "It's true, Etan, so let her be. My father was the Keeper of the Arches, and now, he only has the seventh arch in his charge."

Etan stopped. He shook his massive head as if he didn't hear Lilith correctly. "How…how is this possible?"

The answer hit Lilith as if hundreds of white crawlers were stinging her. *Time. It flows freely, all around us, like the air.* She wasn't supposed to keep time as if it were a thing to store in a box.

Legend of the Timekeepers

She was supposed to preserve and protect time, keep it safe, as her father had told her before they were pulled through the archway. She was supposed to make sure time flowed through her, through everyone, naturally, like breathing in, and breathing out.

"It's possible because time flows through us, Etan," Lilith replied, feeling joy flood her belly. "If you believe what is scribed on the walls of the Temple of the Sun, then you would *know* I'm telling the truth. You would *know* that the Children of the Law of One brought us here to bring back balance. Isn't that enough?"

Etan's olive eyes softened. "If you are here, then Atlantis is truly in trouble."

Lilith nodded. She wouldn't tell them everything. She couldn't.

"How much trouble?" Ajax-ol asked.

"Let's just say, if you have any dreams, you'd better start following them," She-Aba replied.

"I do...have dreams," Ajax-ol said. "I want to build great structures that will last forever." Then his shoulders sagged. "Unfortunately, my dreams are not aligned with my father's plans for me."

Tau grunted, while he stuffed the record keeper inside his leather pouch. "I know what you mean. My father wants me to work on our farm."

"Has something happened that could change our future?" Etan asked, inclining his head.

"Yes," Lilith replied. "Mica, a boy I trusted, tricked me, attacked my father, and entered the seventh Arch of Atlantis uninvited while it was opened to this time. He has come here for a reason, but we don't know why. Our only clue is what Tau scribed in the record keeper."

Etan stroked his goatee. "Then we must do what the Children of the Law of One bid. We must take you to the City of the Golden Gates."

Ajax-ol stiffened. "We? Are you forgetting about your task, Etan? About keeping me safe from the Sons of Belial?"

"The Law of One takes precedence over any task a human gives me," Etan replied.

She-Aba scratched her chin. "I wonder when the first major quake will begin."

A vicious tremor sent shockwaves through Lilith's body and brought her to her knees. A long, pointed crystal hanging over She-

Sharon Ledwith

Aba's head broke away and plunged down toward her. Lilith screamed as Ajax-ol pulled She-Aba away in time. The pair rolled across the cave floor over one another until She-Aba ended on top of him.

"She-Aba! Are you hurt?" Lilith yelled, standing up.

Tau rolled his eyes. "Does she look hurt?"

She-Aba's body was pressed up against Ajax-ol like she was a pearl and he the oyster. She let out a happy sigh just as Ajax-ol awkwardly patted her back. She-Aba propped herself up on her elbows and stared into his face. Her eyes widened. She ran her fingers through his untamed hair. She glanced at Etan, then back down at Ajax-ol, who was now frowning.

"That's it!" she squealed, then snuggled back into Ajax-ol.

"What's it?" Ajax-ol asked, pushing her off.

Giggling, she rolled to her knees. "I know how to keep you safe! The image just popped into my head."

Tau groaned. "Now she's talking crazy and seeing things."

"No, listen. All I need is for Etan to find the carcass of one of those razor-tooth kitties and skin it for its front claws."

Tau snorted. "They're called razor-tooth cats, fire-head!"

She-Aba waved Tau off. "I'll need its tail too if I am to transform Ajax-ol into a human-lion hybrid like Etan." She patted her satchel. "The rest I can do with what's in here."

"You're going to change Ajax-ol's appearance so that he looks like Etan?" Lilith asked. She grinned. "It's a perfect idea! That must be what Istulo meant when she said your life plan indicated illusion and deception, and what Etan said about concealment and hiding things. You are truly an artist with cloth and appearance."

She-Aba beamed. "At least I still get to dress people up."

"Who is Istulo?" Ajax-ol asked, standing up.

"She's the high priestess of the Temple Beautiful in the Black Land," She-Aba replied.

"The Temple Beautiful? It sounds so magnificent," Ajax-ol said dreamily. "I would love to be able to see it someday."

"That's nothing compared to the Great Pyramid!" Tau said, picking up a piece of squashed fruit. "And the Guardian of the Sands is almost completed and ready to be unveiled." He sniffed the fruit, shrugged, and peeled it.

Legend of the Timekeepers

Etan sighed. "Very well, I will find what you've asked for, She-Aba. It is a sound plan." He picked up a crystal shard that resembled a dagger and tested its sharpness.

"But you're forgetting one thing." Lilith clasped her hands. "There's still the problem of finding the One who must banish evil."

Before Etan stepped into the darkness of the forest, he turned and said, "Sometimes we need to trust enough to know that if we follow the scent, the prey will eventually show."

8. The Emissary

"You don't expect me to wear those, do you?" Ajax-ol asked, grimacing.

"I do. Is there a problem?" She-Aba asked, applying white powder to his hands.

"There is still blood on them."

Lilith giggled. "I guess Etan didn't have enough time to wash out the skin properly. But it will help you get into the City of the Golden Gates. Unless—"

"Unless, what?" Ajax-ol cut in.

"Unless you'd rather go back to the forest and fend for yourself," Lilith replied.

Ajax-ol rolled his eyes. "Carry on, She-Aba."

"With pleasure," she said, applying a thin coat of powder to the inside of the razor-tooth cat's skinned paws.

Lilith couldn't believe Ajax-ol's transformation. His skin tone was darkened with a mixture of oils and eye charcoals, his hair was brushed out and waxed to resemble a lion's mane, and his two incisors were fitted with long pieces of thin crystal for fangs. Thankfully Etan had found a dead, half-ravaged razor-tooth cat suitable enough to use for She-Aba's purposes, and skinned it. Its

Legend of the Timekeepers

long, limp tail was stitched into Ajax-ol's linen pants, and She-Aba reminded him to give it life every so often by wiggling his behind.

"Are we ready?" Etan asked, returning from scouting the forest. "All is clear."

He stiffened. His nose twitched.

"Yes, it's me, Etan," Ajax-ol said while She-Aba fitted the claws to his hands.

"Wow, you two look like brothers," Tau said, as he walked up behind Etan. His arms were loaded with more yellow fruit.

Ajax-ol stared at his claws, then touched his face. She-Aba swatted his hands away. "Let the oils cure before you go prodding your face."

"Do I really look like a hybrid?"

"Yes," Etan said. "But you must not forget to act like one."

"How does a hybrid act?" She-Aba asked, putting the powder, charcoals, threads, fish-bone needles, and oils away in her satchel.

Etan grunted. "You must do as humans bid. We were created to serve not rule."

"You make it sound like you're our slaves," Ajax-ol said indignantly. "In our house, we treat our hybrids with dignity."

"You're still labeling Etan as a possession, not a person." Lilith wagged a finger.

Etan sighed. "I know no other life. This is my destiny."

"Maybe you should come to the Black Land and submit yourself to the Temple of Sacrifice, Etan," Tau said, peeling his fruit. "Then you could be free of your fate."

Etan's eyes widened. "Free? How?"

Lilith's jaw dropped. *Uh-oh. If Tau tells him what they do to human-animal hybrids inside the Temple of Sacrifice, he'll think we're worse than savages and won't help us.* She reached over and shoved the yellow fruit in Tau's mouth.

He gagged and sputtered.

"What Tau means—" Lilith scowled at him "—is that you'd be freer than you'd be here. Fewer rules."

She-Aba whacked Tau on the back a few times. "Serves you right for not sharing."

"Has anyone thought of how we're going to find your friend once we're inside the City of the Golden Gates?" Ajax-ol asked.

Tau spit out a chunk of fruit. "Mica is not our friend anymore."

74

Lilith clasped her hands. She thought about the riddle. She thought about her father.

"Why don't we look at the problem as if we were assembling an outfit for a special occasion?" She-Aba said.

"That makes no sense, fire-head," Tau said.

"Not for you, bug-boy, but for someone who has an eye for detail, it does," She-Aba replied, placing her satchel over a shoulder and smoothing her hair.

Lilith released her hands. "Go on."

"What's the one thing Mica did that didn't make sense? Think in terms of mismatching colors or wearing the wrong beads with your outfit."

Tau rolled his eyes. "I don't wear beads, and I always wear the same color."

She-Aba pursed her lips. "Yes, I keep meaning to talk to you about that."

Lilith grazed her bottom lip with her teeth. Everything Mica had done didn't make any sense. Then, she remembered what her father had whispered to her, and Lilith's eyes widened.

"The crystal trident." Lilith arched a fair brow. "Mica took it."

She-Aba snapped her fingers. "Now we're getting somewhere."

"But, the crystal trident is only used to activate the Arch of Atlantis," Lilith said. "It serves no other purpose."

"If he has taken the crystal trident, then there is only one place for him to use it," Etan said.

Ajax-ol stiffened. "Oh, no, not there. Anywhere but there."

"Where?" Tau asked.

Lilith licked her bottom lip. "Mica's going to the innermost circle of the City of the Golden Gates, to the Temple of Poseidon."

"It appears so," Etan said, stroking his goatee.

"Why are you afraid of going there?" She-Aba asked.

"That is where Zurumu serves." Ajax-ol scrunched his face. It made him look more like a baboon than a lion. "And where Belial rules from."

"If Mica is going there, then that's where we must go," Lilith replied with a sharp nod.

Ajax-ol groaned. "Fine. But have you thought of how we are going to get to the Temple of Poseidon?" He snatched up his staff that was leaning against a huge white crystal. "It is surrounded by two separate rings of water."

Legend of the Timekeepers

Etan reached over, took the staff from Ajax-ol, and passed it to Tau. "A hybrid does not carry a staff. And yes, I know of a way. A human-jackal hybrid friend of mine navigates the channels of the City of the Golden Gates on his small ferry. He transports passengers safely through the rings who have business inside the city. Anapa is now free from his bondage to his master and owes me a debt. He will take us."

"What am I supposed to do with this?" Tau asked, staring at the staff.

"I'd tell you to herd goats with it, bug-boy, but since there's none to be found, you could use it to help correct that atrocious posture of yours," She-Aba replied with a smirk.

Lilith stifled a giggle. "In Atlantis, staffs are held by people who have political status or are from the houses of government officials. So if anyone asks, you could say that you represent the House of Duo-She-Dui from the Black Land. My father speaks highly of his accomplishments, and he has roots here in Atlantis."

She-Aba stared at the staff. "I could add some assorted gems and pearls to the staff and give it a thin coat of gold using my face paint to make it look official. Oh, and I'll need your life seal, Tau."

"My life seal?" Tau clapped a hand to his chest, covering his life seal. "No way, fire-head!"

"Come on, Tau, give her your life seal." Lilith nudged him. "She won't ruin it, and it will ensure our safety by saying that you are the scribe of an important emissary sent by Duo-She-Dui like your life seal prophesizes."

Tau's top lip quivered. "What emissary?"

"That...emissary." Lilith pointed to She-Aba.

She-Aba beamed and clapped. "I'm in! I'd be anyone who can boss bug-boy around. I'll get to work to create my costume!"

Tau gingerly removed his life seal. "What about you, Lilith? Who are you going to be?"

Lilith smiled and opened her arms wide. "What you see is what you get. I'm Atlantean. I know our ways and customs, so I'll be able to blend in easily."

"Who is this Duo-She-Dui?" Ajax-ol asked, scratching his palms.

"Duo-She-Dui is a refugee from Atlantis who came to the Black Land many years ago to share his knowledge and teach the beliefs of his culture to our people in the Temple Beautiful," She-Aba replied. "He originally designed and built the Great Pyramid and

76

commissioned the Guardian of the Sands. My father and other members of the high counsel have actually met him."

Ajax-ol sighed. "Seeing as I'm outnumbered, I guess I have no choice."

"Oh, there's always a choice," Lilith said. "My Uncle Kukulkan used to say that no matter how grim things look you still have the power of choice."

Etan smiled that knowing smile. "Are you sure you are not a seer, Lilith?"

"Helping these humans get through the city's rings to the Temple of Poseidon is too dangerous, Etan. What if the temple guards don't believe your friends?"

Etan's broad brow furrowed. "This is what is written and what the Law of One wishes, Anapa, so it shall be done."

Anapa's snout crinkled. Lilith picked out the jackal-like features of this hybrid that made him unique. A long snout. Pointed ears. Dark, rich skin. A closely shaven head. Deep, insightful canine eyes, almost black in color. He wore thick orichalcum bracelets—one on each wrist, both stamped with the Eye of One, and a long, linen skirt fastened with a woven palm leaf sash. In one of his ears was a round, gold earring which sparkled when the sun hit it.

"Very well, old friend, but this will scratch the debt between us." Anapa held out his human hand.

Etan grasped Anapa's hand gently and held it to his heart. "You are released, my friend." Then Etan flinched and rubbed his injured leg that was oozing yellow liquid.

She-Aba smacked his paw away. "Let it be, Etan. The gash needs to breathe and heal without interference."

Tau grunted. "You know, for an emissary, you can be quite bossy, fire-head."

"That's the idea, bug-boy," She-Aba said, grinning. "If I can't play the part of a representative from the House of Duo-She-Dui with confidence, then we won't be able to convince the guards and get through the city safely."

Legend of the Timekeepers

"The girl is correct." Anapa let go of Etan. "I have seen emissaries from other lands come to pay their respects at the Temple of Poseidon. Most command reverence and attention."

Tau smirked. "Oh, She-Aba doesn't need to pretend to command attention. She does that naturally."

Anapa's long ears moved forward. "Your speech sounds broken, unclear. I have something that will take care of that." He bent down to retrieve a satchel from his ferry. "Here, this is for the emissary and her scribe. Wear them and you will be understood clearly."

"A blue crystal hanging on an orichalcum necklace?" Tau asked. "What's that for?"

"I lend these necklaces to visitors from other lands who do not speak our language. The crystal helps us understand them and the visitors to understand Atlanteans." Then Anapa smiled wryly. "It's called a Babel necklace. It cuts the babbling and brings clarity to one's voice."

She-Aba squealed. "I love this, Anapa, thank you! It offsets my outfit perfectly."

"You're wearing a spotted animal skin, fire-head. What's to offset?"

"You know nothing, bug-boy." She-Aba rolled her eyes. "People will be drawn to the necklace, then up toward my face, and be forced to meet me eye to eye."

Tau snorted. "Only if they manage to get past the ridiculous color of your hair."

"Are those two always like that?" Anapa asked.

Etan stroked his beard. "It appears so."

Lilith spotted a group of Atlantean guards detaining six women, all dressed in deep blue gowns, by the main gate of the walled city. A large, white tusked beast tethered by a gold rope on its thick, wrinkled left leg stood behind them. Bundles of fresh food and overstuffed satchels were strapped across the animal's sturdy back. The tusked beast seemed agitated, moving its head to and fro and flapping its big ears as if they were palm leaves waving in the wind. The beast's long snout, the end working like a thumb and finger, reached out to touch the youngest woman on her shoulder. "We'd better get aboard your ferry, Anapa, before those guards get to us," Lilith said, tipping her chin toward the women.

Anapa nodded, then pulled out what looked like a miniature weigh scale from his ferry. It was made of pure silver and had an

78

ivory handle that he gripped tightly. "I'll need a strand of hair from each of you." Anapa held out his scale. "Place it on the left base plate."

"Why?" Tau asked, eyeing the scale suspiciously.

"Anapa must weigh us." Etan pulled out a long, brown hair off the top of his head and placed it on the shiny base plate. "His ferry can take only those who measure."

"Measure?" She-Aba flinched pulling out a red, curly hair.

"To be weighed and measured, even by your hair, determines if I give you a ride," Anapa said. "My former master, Thoth, gave me this scale as a tool for my trade. It has never failed in choosing who I should ferry."

"Here is mine." Lilith unraveled a strand of long blond hair from her finger.

Tau sighed. "Fine. I will do what the Atlanteans do." Then he flinched. "Ouch!"

"Here's bug-boy's limp and unconditioned poor-excuse-for hair," She-Aba said.

Ajax-ol grunted. "This stuff you put in my hair is sticky and thick!"

"It's supposed to be, Ajax-ol," She-Aba said indignantly. "It is bee wax, the best in the Black Land."

Finally yanking a few strands out, his hairs stuck to the palm of his fake paws.

"Here, let me." Lilith pulled apart the strands until one came loose and dropped it on the base plate.

The scale tipped. Anapa went into the satchel he'd retrieved the Babel necklaces from and took out a polished blue stone, flecked with gold, the size of a plump date.

"Ohh, what a beautiful stone!" She-Aba blurted. "It's so flawless."

"It is a rare lapis lazuli I use to weigh matters carefully." Anapa placed the stone on the right base plate. The scale didn't move.

Anapa grunted. "Too much weight."

"Was does that mean?" Tau asked, leaning against Ajax-ol's decorated staff.

"It means not all of you can come." Anapa removed She-Aba's curly red strand from the base plate.

It didn't budge, and he put it back. Apana took another—the long brown hair belonging to Etan. The scale remained the same. Then he

Legend of the Timekeepers

returned it and took Lilith's blond strand. The weight shifted slightly, but not enough to balance the scale. He nodded, flicked her hair to the ground, and picked Ajax-ol's sticky strand. The whole weight shifted until the scales balanced out. His dark eyes became slits, and he attempted a canine smile.

"It is done. The scale is balanced. Lilith and Ajax-ol must be left behind."

"What!" Ajax-ol roared, a little too loud. "But...but I forbid it! You can't do this to me!"

Anapa glared at him. "It is not me doing this to you, but rather the Law of One who determines the way of things. Take it up with the temple priests or priestesses if you have a problem."

Etan pressed his paw on Ajax-ol's shoulder. "All will be well, Ajax-ol, the Law of One wills this."

"Easy for you to say, Etan, you get to go on the ferry." Ajax-ol's shoulders slumped.

Uneasy with the scale's choice too, Lilith slowly looked around for another way into the walled City of the Golden Gates. But there was none. The massive stone walls covered with copper glittered like a serpent's wary eye. Guards were still deterring the women, and their white-tusked beast had calmed down for the moment, though it was now teetering on its two front legs. The sun caught a glimmer of light from the wrist of one woman. Lilith squinted. It was a snake bracelet wrapped around her left forearm. Then she looked over the other women. All wore the same snake bracelet. Lilith's eyes widened. She lightly touched her snake bracelet. *Those women must be seers like my Aunt Ambeno.*

"Etan is right, Ajax-ol, all will be well," Lilith said. "I have a plan that will get us through the gate and across the bridge into the city." She pointed at the seers. "I'll pretend to be a seer from the Black Land and seek immunity with them. It is the code of a seer, to help others on their path. You can act as my servant."

Ajax-ol looked. "I still don't see—" he stopped and his mouth fell open.

"What's the matter with him?" Tau waved a hand in front of Ajax-ol's face.

"Not what, but who." Etan pointed toward the youngest seer.

Lilith guessed the woman must be close to her eighteenth year. Her fair skin shone like glass. She had high cheekbones, a slender, regal nose, and hair the color of glittering alabaster, bound with a

80

pearl headpiece. Her tall, willow-like frame made the rich, blue gown she was wearing hug her body naturally.

"Rhea," Ajax-ol whispered. "I...I thought I would never see her again."

"Well, now's your chance," Lilith said, pulling his arm.

He stiffened. "I can't let her see me like this!"

"Well, you can't let her see you in your human form," She-Aba said. "That would be stupid. And stupid is something Tau would do."

Tau grunted. He opened his mouth just as Anapa covered it with his hand. "Let it be and get on the ferry, the pair of you."

"Still don't have the patience for foreigners, I see," Etan said, smiling his knowing smile. "You should have never gotten into this ferry business."

Anapa shrugged. "It is what I know, Etan. It is who I am."

"Ajax-ol, we can get into the City of the Golden Gates without the others. Have enough faith to know this." Lilith pulled his arm harder. She looked at Tau and She-Aba. "Go on, we'll be fine. I'm on my home soil now."

She-Aba sighed. She wagged a finger at Ajax-ol. "And don't forget to give your tail a wiggle."

He grunted. "It will probably be the only way it doesn't get stepped on."

She-Aba smiled, then lunged for Lilith. She hugged her fiercely. "Be careful"

"I will," Lilith said, hugging her back.

"If you think I'm going to hug you, Atcha-girl, you'll be waiting until the next flood."

Lilith laughed. "If you think about it, Tau, that's only one hundred years from now."

Legend of the Timekeepers

Sharon Ledwith

9. The Prophecy

"*I* think this is a big mistake," Ajax-ol said, watching the ferry leave.

Lilith nudged him. "There are no mistakes. Get that through your thick skull. Come on, before the seers are allowed entrance."

"I didn't know there was a House of Seers established in the Black Land." Ajax-ol scratched his paws. Flies were starting to buzz around them as they got closer to the women.

"There is now." Lilith pushed her snake bracelet up her arm and adjusted her seashell belt. "And stop scratching your hands, the seers will think you have a plague."

Ajax-ol frowned. "I do. She's blond, thin, and full of herself."

Lilith waved off the flies. "At least you still have your humor underneath all that make-up and wax."

"She-Aba would make for a better torturer."

Lilith giggled. An Atlantean guard immediately stood in front of her. Lilith banged into him, and she stumbled. Ajax-ol caught her before she fell.

"Back of the line with you two," he said with a tone of authority.

Shaken, Lilith stared up at the monstrous guard. He wore a tall helmet embellished with feathers and a golden breastplate over a

83

Legend of the Timekeepers

linen tunic. The breastplate was stamped with a trident. A dagger was fastened on the upper part of each arm with a jeweled band. By his side, a large brown shaggy dog with alert dark eyes and a blue tongue held its position next to its master.

"You imbecile!" Ajax-ol shouted.

The guard balked. "What did you say, lion-face?"

His dog growled, baring its teeth. Its massive paw struck the ground.

Lilith heard Ajax-ol gulp. He grinned and wiggled his limp tail.

A small movement on the ground caught her eye. A rodent darted from a crate of sweet-smelling fruit to an open satchel left on the ground by a woman awaiting entrance into the city. The white-tusked beast must have seen the rodent too. The beast raised its long snout and bellowed out an ominous low cry that sounded like it originated from its belly. Frightened, the tusked beast backed up with enough force to drag the young seer Ajax-ol had called Rhea by its rope. She struggled, then collapsed. Her knees scraped along the ground, but she continued to hold on.

Screams rose from the people who were awaiting passage through the gate. Some ran away, others jumped in the nearby rushing water. Guards started to circle the unruly tusked beast, their spears up and pointing toward it. The seers shouted at the guards, pleading for them to put down their weapons and move away. The guard hovering above Lilith and Ajax-ol abruptly left them and rushed over to join the other guards. His dog snapped and lunged at the seer's beast, its master letting out the leash enough to scare the tusked beast into backing farther away.

"Rhea!" Ajax-ol yelled. "Let go!"

The tusked beast raised its white, long snout into the air and bugled. Lilith could feel its fear run rampant through her, as if they were connected in that moment. Her limbs shook, her heart raced, and her lips trembled. Lilith's eyes widened. *If I can sense the tusked beast's feelings, then surely it can sense mine.* She set her jaw. Enough was enough. The guards were taunting this poor beast, baiting it, treating this like a cruel, blood thirsty game that would only end in the death of the seer's beast. Her body tensed as Lilith stamped her foot and screamed, "Cowards! You shame Atlantis! You defy Poseidon!"

Then Lilith pushed her way through two guards and turned to face them. Without saying another word, she dug her bare feet into the rich volcanic soil, opened her arms wide, and concentrated all her thoughts on the frightened tusked beast behind her, ignoring all surrounding noises. A deep sense of calm overrode her and the beast. The barrier was gone between them, and Lilith felt a connection to it, like she and this creature of nature were linked, were one. *Stop swaying, stop pulling, be still, be calm,* she thought. *You are safe. Trust me.*

She suddenly felt something cool, soft, and wet on her cheek. The end of the tusked beast's long snout smelled her, touched her, and nuzzled her. Lilith knew it trusted her on a level only she could understand. She reached for the pink end of its snout and placed it on her chest, letting the creature feel the fast, steady beats of her heart. A satisfied groan coupled with relief, like the sound a child would make after finding a lost parent in a crowd, emerged from the tusked beast. She stroked its snout with her thumb, giving it confirmation and strength.

The Atlantean guards grumbled amongst themselves, lowered their spears, and backed away. Even the dog stopped barking and snapping. It lowered its hackles and whined. Most of the guards retreated to one of the sparkling observation towers flanking the bridge.

"Elie trusts you."

Startled, Lilith turned around. Rhea smiled at her. Her knees were scraped and her gown wrinkled and dirty. Lilith smiled back. "I trust her too. She'll be fine. I think she just needed reassurance."

"I believe she has that now," Rhea said. "How did you calm her so easily?"

Lilith shrugged. "I…I'm not sure." She toyed with her snake bracelet. "It came on suddenly, this urge to protect her."

"An earth mind-link," the oldest seer said, trundling up behind them. Lilith noticed she was cross-eyed, and her long hair was as white as the clouds. "You used the earth's power to send positive vibrations to the beast. You understand the language of One. Very impressive, child. I haven't seen that technique used since I was an initiate."

Lilith blinked. *Earth mind-link? Language of One?* She had heard of such gifts. Her Aunt Ambeno had mastered many of the aspects of connecting with nature. But Lilith never dreamed it was possible to possess this ability to link with the earth on a higher level without any formal training.

Legend of the Timekeepers

"Are you all right, Rhea?" Ajax-ol pushed his way through the crowd. His eyes were wide, his breathing ragged. Flies buzzed around him.

Rhea arched her brow. "Have we met?"

"No." Lilith scowled at Ajax-ol. She waved him off. "I…I told him your name. I am Lilith…a seer from the Black Land. This is—" *Wait. I can't say his real name.* Lilith's mind raced in circles until she blurted, "—Tau. My servant."

"Tau?" Ajax-ol and Rhea replied together.

Lilith stroked Elie's snout. She didn't know many boys in the Black Land so she chose the first name that popped into her head, since Tau annoyed her as much as the flies were bothering Ajax-ol. She nudged him. "Is something wrong with your hearing? Do you have wax in your ears, *Tau*?"

"Probably," he muttered, pulling at his sticky hair. He sighed, then placed his paws together and bowed to Rhea. "Forgive me. I was concerned."

"How do you know Rhea's name?" the old seer asked, pursing her thin lips to one side. Her eyes moved around like they were immersed in a bowl of water.

"I…I foresaw meeting her," Lilith blurted. "In…in a dream." She dug her feet deeper into the cool, dark earth. Oddly, this felt comfortable, like being wrapped in a silk sheet.

The old seer's eyes rolled around again. She placed a finger in the middle of her forehead, then she grasped Lilith's left arm and stared at her snake bracelet intensely. Lilith felt her warm breath on her arm, smelled the sweetness of her skin. "The girl speaks the truth." She dropped her hand from her head. "This piece is indeed ancient. Only those who pass several initiations may wear this unique bracelet. I believe her. She has come to us for a reason."

A guard with a trident stamped on his tall helmet approached them. He had a tattoo of a serpent around his neck. Lilith knew this marked him Captain of the Guards. "You are free to enter the City of the Golden Gates. Your scrolls are in order. Belial is expecting you."

Lilith's eyes widened. *Belial is expecting these seers?*

The old seer placed her hands together and bowed slightly. Lilith heard her back crack. "Thank you. I shall send a special protection prayer to Poseidon for you and your men."

86

A short, but powerful, tremor shook the ground. People behind them screamed out for their gods' mercy and protection. The surge went through Lilith's legs and into her belly. Elie placed her long snout on Lilith's stomach, and she released a visceral noise to let Lilith know she wasn't imagining these strange new sensations that connected her to the earth.

The captain grunted. "It'll take more than your prayers to Poseidon to halt the instability in Atlantis, Shu-Tu."

Shu-Tu shrugged. "They can't hurt either." Then she turned to the other four seers stationed behind Elie. "Prepare yourselves. We take our leave. Atlantis needs us."

Lilith had been through the entrance of the City of the Golden Gates more times than she could remember. Her father had told her the city had been rebuilt at least four times over after earthquakes and volcanic eruptions severely damaged their beloved city. And the Atlanteans always rebuilt in the same pattern—circles of land surrounded by three rings of water. *Circular motion is the law of everything,* her mother, a teacher of the sacred laws, had once shared with her. Lilith swallowed hard. Soon, all this would be destroyed and there would be no more rebuilding.

A timber and marble bridge, inlaid with gleaming metals and precious stones, led them across the canal into the outermost city ring. A pang of sadness went through Lilith like a knife. She cast her eyes around the ring, comprised mostly of a giant race track used to entertain hard-working Atlanteans. She spied a line of golden chariots racing in the distance, their sleek dark horses digging into the dirt, connecting to it as she had done.

Ajax-ol was instructed to lead Elie. He didn't appear too happy about, but he couldn't argue. Hybrids were not afforded that luxury. The seer's white beast didn't seem to mind Ajax-ol, and at times playfully stuck the end of her snout in his sticky hair and pulled at it. He waved her off. She'd grab his droopy tail. He smacked her snout away. She whacked the back of his head. This made Rhea laugh.

Lilith caught him grinning under his makeup. She rolled her eyes. Ajax-ol must really like Rhea if he continued to allow Elie to poke at him. They passed through the first ring easily, going across another timber and marble bridge shimmering with jewels, and headed toward the second wall of the city. Unlike the first wall covered in copper, this one was coated with tin. The ancient

Legend of the Timekeepers

alchemists of Atlantis had chosen the metals wisely, each possessing the ability to energetically connect with the planets and stars.

Once they passed the gate, Rhea suddenly started to sing. Her voice sounded lyrical, magical. Lilith's whole body relaxed to the rhythm of her voice. She tingled all over, and the hairs on her arms and neck quivered like the effect a crystal bowl had on her when it was played. Lilith sighed. Rhea's song reminded her of how much she missed the special healing concerts the city had offered as a way of calming the people through the numerous eruptions and tremors of their country. Many of the citizens of the city stopped what they were doing and listened, some approached bearing fruit to give to her. Rhea accepted their offerings with a bow, not missing a single beat, and passed most of the fruit to Elie. She let out a low rumbling sound in appreciation, her long snout greedily shoving the food into her mouth.

"Rhea's voice…it's like nothing I've ever heard before," Lilith whispered, not wanting to interrupt the enchantment.

"Yes," Ajax-ol muttered. "It is a rare gift she possesses. The unique tones and pitches in her voice allow her to create perfect harmony between humans and nature. She is truly an instrument to be used for the highest good of Atlantis. The Law of One has blessed her."

Lilith caught the tone of pride in Ajax-ol's voice. She nudged him. "Is she your special one?"

"I…I wish it were that simple." He stared at the glittering ground.

"How so?"

Ajax-ol shrugged. "My family has chosen someone else for me. I have my path. Rhea has hers."

"Sometimes paths meet," Lilith replied, patting his arm. She waved away flies buzzing around his paws and tail.

"As long as I remain in Atlantis, our paths will grow farther apart. That is the way of things. Let it be. I have learned to live with it."

Lulled back to Rhea's alluring singing, Lilith wiped a trickle of sweat rolling down her cheek and fanned her face. It was getting warmer, the air thick with moisture. Fragrant smells of incense burning in nearby circular homes constructed of red, black, and white stones roused her in a nostalgic way. Children laughed and played outside, chasing each other in a game of kickball. Fruit and nut trees shaded some of the houses while vines with blooms the size of melons covered the outside walls of other round buildings.

The whole city shimmered when the sun touched it. Lilith hooded her eyes. The opulence of the City of the Golden Gates was like nothing she'd ever seen in any other place. And probably would never see again. Orichcalcum was plentiful and used as trim for homes and temples. Flat-topped pyramids were positioned throughout the city, all built on higher ground. Crystals the size of Elie's head adorned every pyramid's summit. The deeper they walked into the city, the steeper the land became. Every now and then, Lilith would scan the canal looking for a glimpse of Anapa's ferry.

They had almost reached the inner circle and the final wall of the city. This wall was bathed entirely in orichalcum. It sparkled like a raging fire in the midst of changing direction, projecting the simultaneous feelings of a warning and an auspicious welcome for Lilith's return home. Rhea stopped singing, severing the connection she had created with all those around her. Lilith shivered and clasped her hands.

"Why do you wish to meet with Belial, Shu-Tu?" Lilith asked, breaking the silence between them.

"Your dream did not reveal this to you?" she replied warily.

"No," Lilith replied, tired of lying. "All I know is that we were sent here to return the One who must banish evil, before the end of the first major quake."

Shu-Tu held her hand out to the other seers to stop them. "You know."

"Know what?"

"You know of the impending doom. You know of the prophecy. You are the Timekeeper."

Lilith sighed and unclasped her hands. She reached under the neckline of her gown and pulled out her life seal to show Shu-Tu and the other seers. Rhea gasped. She placed her hands together and bowed reverently. "We have been foretold of your coming."

The four other seers placed their hands together and bowed too. Lilith heard them mutter a prayer to Poseidon. Confused, she shook her head. "All I know is that we were sent here by the Children of the Law of One to complete a task."

"Then that is all you need to know," Shu-Tu replied. "That knowledge is enough for now."

Legend of the Timekeepers

"So how—" Lilith paused, trying to form the correct words "—will I know what needs to happen next to carry out the Law of One's wishes?"

"You don't," Rhea replied. "You look, listen, and trust. That is all any of us can do."

"You must open your mind, child," Shu-Tu said. She reached out to touch Lilith in the center of the forehead. "Deep, inner knowledge comes from this place. Learn to open this area, to receive what needs to be received, and the answer will come."

Shu-Tu's eyes moved around, looking this way and that way, focusing but not focusing. "Do not allow your fears to cloud this area, Lilith. Fears can cripple a person just as they can cripple a country." She removed her finger from Lilith's forehead and looked around before she said, "Fears need to be removed from the mind so that insights may be received. In any matter, you must learn to dig deep within yourself, remove the illusion, and seek the truth. This will set you free."

"But how will this help Lilith return the One who must banish evil?" Ajax-ol asked, adjusting the rope around Elie's thick, wrinkled leg. She smacked him with her long snout.

Shu-Tu arched her white brows. Her eyes spun around her sockets. "You were not spoken to, Tau."

"But, this one seems different, Shu-Tu," Rhea said. "Perhaps the people of the Black Land allow certain liberties for their hybrids. Perhaps we should listen to what he has to say."

Lilith sighed. "Permission to speak, Tau."

"You say Lilith must remove illusion and seek the truth," Ajax-ol said, scratching at his paws. "You say she is the one Atlantis has been waiting for. I say you're expecting too much from this girl. It is up to Atlanteans to wake up to the abomination of the Sons of Belial. This crisis did not happen overnight."

"No, it did not," Shu-Tu replied. "But who is to say it cannot be corrected by tomorrow? This is the power of hope and faith. You need to understand that."

Ajax-ol grunted. "It would take the forces of Poseidon to correct what Belial and his Black Priests have done here."

"Precisely," Shu-Tu said. "The earthquakes and eruptions are Poseidon's way of letting Belial and his followers know just how displeased he is. They will either get worse or get better."

Sharon Ledwith

"What if they get worse?" Lilith asked. "What does the prophecy say about that?"

Rhea placed her slim hand on Lilith's shoulder. "The prophecy is clouded. That is why we asked for an audience with Belial."

"You asked to see Belial?" Lilith turned to look Rhea in the eye. "What do you hope to gain from him?"

"Clarity," Shu-Tu said. "If nothing changes, then everything changes."

Ajax-ol sighed. "Then let's hope for change."

Rhea giggled. "Change is the only constant, Tau."

Legend of the Timekeepers

10. Belial

"Ohhh, it's exactly how I remembered it," Lilith said, with a hint of longing. "So beautiful, so grand."

"You make it sound like you haven't visited here in a long time," Ajax-ol whispered.

"I…I haven't."

Lilith stared up at the Temple of Poseidon situated on the highest point of the city. Made of the whitest and purest marble, and trimmed with shiniest orichalcum, it resembled a gleaming pearl in an oyster to her. It would take a line of at least twenty tusked beasts to measure this magnificent structure's length, and twenty-five stacked on top of each other to judge the height. Brilliant marble steps were cut into the hill, winding upwards as if the Atlantean craftsmen had followed a serpent's trail. Then Lilith looked around. Blue tiles, polished to the highest luster, covered the grounds of the courtyard below the temple. Flowing fountains were everywhere, offering people sanctuary from the heat and a place to congregate. A succession of golden statues, all former kings and their wives, held their position among the flowering shrubs and lofty trees. Silver snakes surrounded the base of each statue, their eyes glittering with gemstones the size and color of ripened olives. Elie raised her long

Legend of the Timekeepers

snout and bugled, then headed for the closest fountain, scattering peacocks in her wake.

Ajax-ol stumbled and fell. At least he had enough sense to let go of the rope.

"Are you hurt, Tau?" Rhea helped him up. She was trying not to laugh.

Ajax-ol grinned. "I'm not now."

"Your claws, they…they look infected," she said, pointing. "You keep scratching them. And the flies are attracted to the smell. That is not good. Your tail seems lifeless too. Perhaps I could give you a healing powder for relief?"

"Um…sure, yes, that would be kind of you." Ajax-ol wiggled his behind. "But…but first, Elie needs food. I shall lead her to the grassy knoll near the canal."

Ajax-ol bowed to Rhea, then turned and ran after Elie, who was now spraying herself all over using her powerful long snout. Some of the mist landed on a group of priests dressed completely in black robes. Lilith's eyes widened. *Uh-oh, not on the Black Priests, Elie!* One bellowed out a vulgar word Lilith had heard her uncle utter only once when he and her father were discussing Belial.

"Augh! Who owns this disgusting tusked beast?" a Black Priest shrieked.

"Hello, Bus-Lu," Shu-Tu said, her voice void of any emotion. "She belongs to us."

"Shu-tu? Weren't you banished from the Temple of Poseidon?"

"Yes, I was," she replied stoically. "Belial is expecting us."

Lilith's stomach cramped. The Black Priest Shu-Tu had called Bus-Lu strutted toward them, his robe unfurling like a vulture's wings. His dark gray hair was pleated and tied back, making his plump clean-shaven face look like a melon. Oddly, his eyes matched the color of his hair. Black Priests had always had a reputation of being above all others, of answering to no one except Belial. And judging by this Black Priest's manner, Lilith knew that nothing about him was reverent. "Expecting you? What game are you playing here, Shu-Tu?" Bus-Lu asked, exposing his uneven teeth. "Seers are no longer welcome here."

"I play no games, Bus-Lu. I only bring Belial news of the prophecy."

94

Bus-Lu wiped his damp chin. "Tell me. I will relay your message to Belial. Your ridiculous spinning eyeballs will only serve to distract and make him laugh."

Lilith heard guffaws coming from the fountain. At least Ajax-ol had managed to lead Elie away from the rest of the Black Priests.

"I seek his audience, not yours, Bus-Lu." Shu-Tu's eyes rapidly moved from side to side. Then she went cross-eyed and grinned. "Now go back to lurking in Belial's shadow, you poor excuse for a priest."

Bus-Lu growled. "You dare to insult a Black Priest? Guards! Surround the tusked beast and bring it to the temple! It will take the bull's place for tonight's sacrifice!"

"Nooo!" Rhea screamed, falling to her knees.

Temple guards, with breastplates made of orichalcum, circled Elie and Ajax-ol and waved their gold-tipped spears in the air. An archer pulled out of the ranks and readied his bow with a silver-tipped arrow. Ajax-ol held tightly to Elie's rope while patting her leg in an attempt to keep her calm. Elie began to teeter. She flapped her huge ears, raised her long snout, and cried out a warning.

Panicking, Lilith found a freshly tilled garden next to a circle of giant white crystal stones. She dug her feet into the soil until she could only see the tops of them. Then Lilith opened her arms wide, closed her eyes, and concentrated. *Please, please, please, protect Elie, please, please, please!*

"Release the tusked beast!"

Lilith opened her eyes. *I know that voice.* "She-Aba?"

"Make way for the Emissary of Duo-She-Dui from the Black Land," Tau announced, holding Ajax-ol's gilded staff in front of him. His life seal swung proudly from the top of the staff.

"What's the meaning of this? Who is Duo-She-Dui?" Bus-Lu snapped, turning to face She-Aba.

Lilith looked behind her friends. Both Etan and Anapa were tying the ferry to a dappled marble dock. Anapa appeared nervous, his pointy ears lowered. However, Etan seemed more at ease, his shoulders down and body relaxed. They must have concocted this plan on the way here. She noticed a swarm of flies gathering around his wounded leg. This didn't seem to bother Etan, as he remained focused on securing the ferry.

She-Aba swished a hand in the air. "Silence! To not know Duo-She-Dui insults not only my people but your people as well."

Legend of the Timekeepers

Lilith smiled. She-Aba was taking her role as an emissary seriously. Lilith noticed She-Aba seemed taller. She looked down, and her eyes widened. She-Aba had on a new pair of shoes. These were higher than any of her other creations and decorated with strips of orichalcum and colored gems. She'd also crafted her life seal into a fancy brooch which held the spotted animal skin she wore in place. She-Aba sauntered over to stand before Bus-Lu. Her shoes gave her the advantage height-wise. Tau joined her. He banged the staff three times on the ground, reached into his leather pouch, and produced a small scroll. He handed it to She-Aba, who opened it. Her eyes bugged. She passed it back to Tau.

"I cannot read your scribble, Scribe. You read it," she said flatly.

Tau rolled his eyes. He cleared his throat, and said, "By decree of the House of Duo-She-Dui, we come bearing an important message from the people of the Black Land."

Bus-Lu laughed, his fat throat bulging to twice its size. "The House of Duo-She-Dui sends children to the Temple of Poseidon? No wonder the Black Land is full of savages and fools!"

The other Black Priests howled with laughter, slapping each other's backs. Even the temple guards snickered. Lilith clasped her hands. This wasn't going in their favor. What were She-Aba and Tau up to? Barely controlling his laughter, Bus-Lu waved to his fellow priests to be silent. He smirked and said, "So what is this important message that the House of Duo-She-Dui sends children to deliver?"

The guards had lowered their spears, some leaning against them, in anticipation of hearing what Tau had to say. Lilith's toes started to tingle. This sensation moved through her feet and surged up her legs. Releasing her hands, Lilith let the earth talk to her, link to her, and connect with her in a way she'd never known before. *Be prepared,* a voice whispered to her.

She jerked. "Be prepared for what?"

"This message, melon-head!" Tau said as he dropped the scroll and raised the staff. He walloped Bus-Lu on top of his head. Crack! Bus-Lu screamed, collapsed to his knees, and coddled his head like a precious golden egg.

Lilith's mouth dropped. She wasn't prepared for that. "Tau!"

"Yes?" Tau and Ajax-ol said in unison.

Lilith groaned.

96

"There are two Taus?" Rhea asked, standing. "This…this cannot be chance."

"Archer! Kill the human-jackal hybrid who brought these scourges from the Black Land here!" Bus-Lu yelled, trying to stand. Dizzy with pain, he fell again.

Before Lilith took her next breath, an arrow flew at Anapa. Etan roared, pushed his friend into the canal, and took the arrow for his friend. He grasped the arrow protruding from his stomach, threw back his shaggy head, and roared with enough power to scatter a flock of birds resting in a nearby tree. Then Etan stumbled and plummeted to the ground.

"Etan!" Ajax-ol screamed. He dropped Elie's rope and sprinted toward him.

Before the archer had time to nock another arrow, Tau poked him in the stomach with the staff, then struck him across the chest. He stumbled backward and fell into the closest fountain. "And that's for Etan, serqet-breath!"

Panicking, Lilith clapped her hands together three times, then opened her arms wide, letting all her foreboding feelings seep into the ground. She closed her eyes. *Use me. Show me what I need to know, and what I need to do.* Suddenly, a small, but significant tremor shot through her toes and up her legs. She opened her eyes and smiled. *Thank you. I know what to do.*

Concentrating all her thoughts on Elie, Lilith began to sway, moving her hands back and forth, like branches caught up in the wind. Her body spiraling in, spiraling out. Slow at first, she gained momentum, while her whole body swayed, rocked, and wavered with the language of the earth. Elie mimicked Lilith, her huge body moving to and fro, her snout swinging, her tusks cutting into the air. Lilith directed Elie toward the attacking guards on her left. Elie scooped them up with her long tusks and pitched them into the canal. Turning, the great white beast picked up the remaining guards and heaved them into the tree tops. Most had either lost their spears in the canal or were caught in the branches. Elie raised her long nose and trumpeted a victory cry.

Lilith released her bond with the earth and ran toward Etan and Ajax-ol. Anapa had managed to pull himself out of the canal and stood dripping over them, with his ears forward and his eyes solemn. Anapa's earring glittered, catching the sun in an unusual way so that it shone down on Etan's face. He was smiling that

Legend of the Timekeepers

knowing smile. His breathing was deep and labored. Blood covered both his paws and seeped into the ground. He looked directly at Lilith for a moment and his smile deepened.

"Timekeeper," he strained to say, "you know what to do. You know what you are capable of now. My purpose here is done."

Lilith jerked. "You knew? All this time, you knew?"

Etan nodded in silence.

"No, no, no, Etan." Ajax-ol cradled Etan's head in his lap. "The seers are here, they…they know of remedies that will heal your arrow wound."

Lilith licked her lips. "The wyvern. It…it poisoned you, didn't it?"

Etan nodded slowly. "I took in the poison, so that you, your friends, and Ajax-ol may live."

"But…but the tail never touched him," Ajax-ol said in a broken voice.

"The back claw did," Etan replied weakly. "It's…it's tipped with a slow-acting poison."

"Did…did I hear you correctly?" Rhea asked as she walked up behind them. Elie's rope was in her hands. "Did you just call Tau, Ajax-ol?"

Ajax-ol sighed. "Yes, Rhea, it's me." He pulled off the fly-infested paws, then ripped away the tail She-Aba had fashioned for him and cast them aside.

"Why would you pose as a human-lion hybrid?" She squeezed the gold rope in her hands so tight her knuckles turned white.

A laugh sounding like a snake's warning hiss echoed behind them. "Because Ajax-ol, son of Ajxor, is a coward. And cowards tend to hide in sheep's clothing."

Lilith glanced over her shoulder. Her jaw dropped. She'd seen many drawings and carvings of him before. Statues were erected all over this city by his followers. Her throat tightened at her first real glimpse of him, this magus, this monster.

Belial loomed before them, his shadow engulfing Etan's face like a hungry viper. Tall and lean, his straight nose overpowered his long face and small ears. A corkscrew-braided beard covered his entire chest, and his shoulder-length dark brown curly hair was held in place by a purple headband with an orichalcum snake's head protruding from it. Lilith shivered. Even being in this dark magus's shadow was enough to snuff her light out.

"Move aside," She-Aba yelled, pushing her way past the guards flanking Belial. Tau was two steps behind her, holding up Ajax-ol's staff, which he'd recently turned into a weapon. "I am the Emissary of the House of Duo-She-Dui from the Black Land. I demand an audience!"

Belial's dark brows narrowed. Then he spotted Tau's life seal swinging from the staff. He snatched it in mid-air and stared at it. His onyx-colored eyes widened. He glared at She-Aba and reached for her life seal brooch. A sinister smile fissured from his thin lips. "There is another one here with a talisman like these. Show yourself, or these two will be sacrificed now!"

"Sacrificed?" Tau shouted indignantly. "Don't we get diplomatic immunity?"

"But I have red hair!" She-Aba snapped her fingers. "Doesn't that give me goddess status around here?"

Belial snickered. "Alas, no. You both have been sadly misinformed. But if you'd like, I can arrange a clean, quick death. No entrails, no mess."

Lilith clasped her hands. "No, wait! Please, spare them. I have one!"

Belial released her friends' life seals. He turned, making his shimmering purple robe swirl around his thin ankles. He beckoned her over with a long spindly finger.

Lilith gulped. Before she could walk over to him, Etan grabbed her foot. Startled, she looked down. Life was draining from his eyes, yet he still smiled that knowing smile. "You are not alone in this, Lilith. You...you have...the unseen power...inside you...to face...each obstacle...you meet. So...do...your...friends." He paused to take one last breath. "Remember...this. Trust...this. Know...this." Then Etan's olive eyes rolled back, and he lay still.

"Etan! No, no, no!" Ajax-ol sobbed, burying his face in Etan's mane.

Anapa lowered to one knee and brushed his hand over Etan's eyes to close them.

Bus-Lu laughed wickedly, rubbing his head. "I'm surprised at you, Shu-Tu. For being a seer, you never saw this coming."

Shu-Tu smiled. Her eyes rolled around at an accelerated rate, then crossed. "Bus-Lu, you are as blind as ever. There is the known and the unknown. And then, there is the unknowable."

Legend of the Timekeepers

Sharon Ledwith

11. *Serpents and Spirals*

"**H**ow…how could you have known about us?" Lilith asked in a low, guarded voice.

"Such a pointless question, girl," Belial replied, revealing a polished incisor. "The answer is how could I have not?"

With the point of his bejeweled dagger, Belial lifted Lilith's dangling life seal from under the neckline of her gown. She swallowed hard and eyed Belial, this Thirteenth Magus of the Arcane Tradition, who specialized in sorcery of the darkest kind. Necromancy. Senseless sacrifice. Black magic.

His nostrils flared like a raging bull. "Spirals," he said, though it sounded like the hiss of a snake to Lilith. His breath reeked of mint and garlic.

"The power of nature," Lilith replied bravely. Her throat loosened, allowing her to breathe easier.

Belial laughed wickedly, making the hairs on Lilith's neck ripple. "You know nothing, girl, nothing of nature. Spirals are the power of all things."

"Why would someone like you care about our life seals?"

"Life seals? Is that what you call them?" Belial shrugged. "I don't care. At least not anymore."

101

Legend of the Timekeepers

Lilith frowned. "Not anymore?"

"You and those Black Land savages are no longer a threat to me," he replied, wagging the dagger in her face. "My high priestess Zurumu is to be commended, and she will be rewarded handsomely for her insight."

"What insight?" Lilith clasped her hands together. She tried to dig her feet into the ground, but it was rock hard.

Belial tapped the dagger under her chin. A steely chill went through Lilith. "Zurumu had a dream. It was foretold to her that travelers wearing talismans from the Black Land will come here to disrupt Atlantis. Amongst them, one will carry the spiral power. Zurumu informed me this traveler will be the most dangerous, and that none of them are to be trusted."

"Zurumu!" Ajax-ol roared. "She is the cause of this? She is the one not to be trusted!"

"Hold your tongue, Ajax-ol!" Belial spat. "Or I'll cut it out myself."

"Belial," Shu-Tu spoke up, as she cautiously approached him. "There is still the matter of the prophecy to discuss. Atlantis's future depends upon it."

"Why should I be concerned with anything the seers who follow the Children of the Law of One have to say, hag?" Belial sneered.

"If you do not listen, then soon there will be no place for you to rule from, Belial," Shu-Tu replied. "It is as simple as that."

A sudden rumble shook the earth, making Lilith's stomach heave. Her feet burned as if she were standing in a pit full of red coals. Birds scattered to the air, and Elie nervously moved from side to side, like she was compensating for the imbalance of this place. A statue of a former king fell off its pedestal. The head broke off and rolled across the tiles to land near Belial. The tremors lasted through three of Lilith's short breaths, then ceased. Her feet instantly cooled.

Belial's face twitched like he'd been bitten by a white crawler. "Very well, Shu-Tu, you will have your audience." Then he narrowed his brow. "And I will have my sacrifice."

"No hybrids in the Temple of Poseidon!" a guard shouted, holding a spear at Ajax-ol's throat. "It is forbidden!"

Sharon Ledwith

Bus-Lu waved the guard aside. "Imbecile, look closer. This boy hides behind a child's mask." He roughly wiped some of the make-up away from Ajax-ol's face with the back of his hand. "He is here for Belial's judgment."

"I believe he's already been judged in your eyes, Bus-Lu," Shu-Tu said, calmly. "At least he had the courage to stand up for what he believes in."

"If anyone should be wearing a mask, it's that pasty-faced Black Priest," She-Aba muttered to Lilith.

"Should have whacked him harder," Tau grumbled.

Lilith stifled a giggle.

Bus-Lu spun around, glaring. He shook Ajax-ol's staff that he had seized from Tau. "Silence! You are about to enter sacred ground!"

Shu-Tu walked past the guard and up the marble stairs. Rhea and the other seers followed. "Do not make me laugh, Bus-Lu," she replied over her shoulder. "This place hasn't been sacred for a very long time."

Carefully guarded from all sides, Lilith, She-Aba, Tau, and Ajax-ol were led up the stairs to the threshold of the Temple of Poseidon. Columns coated in orichalcum and adorned with serpents and vessels and tridents greeted them like glittering giants. Above the entrance loomed an orichalcum arch with a gold statue of Belial perched on the top. To Lilith, he resembled a hungry vulture with his hook nose and arms spread apart awaiting more victims. The vast inner compound opened up to them like a monstrous mouth with marble stairs and gleaming white pillars on each side. Across the compound, a line of smaller golden statues of Atlantis's past kings stood on both sides of a set of wide, marble stairs leading to the second tier of the temple.

Lilith's eyes widened. There was no crack in the stairs leading up to the second tier. She knew these stairs well, had climbed them more times than she could count. The Arches of Atlantis were housed in the second tier. This is where her father received the messages from the Children of the Law of One. This is where he relayed those messages to the king. And this is where the Black Priests ruled from. Her eyes moved up to the third and final tier of the temple. She'd never been invited in there. That tier was only reserved for the king and his advisors. And now for Belial, the blackest priest of all.

103

Legend of the Timekeepers

Lilith's breath caught in her chest as she peered over her shoulder before they were herded into the compound of the first level of the Temple of Poseidon. Anapa had wrapped Etan's body up in the dark cover he used to protect his ferry from the rains and had placed him in the boat. Belial had commanded Anapa's boat to be set on fire before he left to make preparations to receive Lilith, She-Aba, Tau, Ajax-ol, and the seers inside the temple. Lilith stiffened. Belial's cruel order would leave Anapa without the purpose he had been bred for—the worst possible punishment for a hybrid. Elie had been chained to a tree with a base the size of a temple's column. Lilith exhaled. There would be no escaping for her. Lilith rocked back and forth. Without the earth beneath her feet, she felt as chained and confined as Elie.

Four huge soldiers stepped in front of the lead temple guard once they were inside. The guard bowed on one knee in front of the tallest soldier and motioned for the other guards to take their leave. All the guards who escorted them up to the Temple of Poseidon swiftly retreated down the winding stairs. Unnerved by this reaction, Lilith looked up at the soldiers. There was something odd about them, something not right. All were captains, each with a tattooed serpent surrounding his neck. All wore helmets stamped with three tridents. All wore a gold breastplate over a black linen tunic and carried orichalcum spears. But there was no facial expression on them. Their eyes, vacant of life, stared back at Lilith and her friends. Their skin was leathery and pallid. A wiggling movement on the soldiers' arms startled Lilith. Her mouth opened, and she took a step back. Slithering snakes were wrapped around their muscular biceps, held in place by a jewel-embellished black band.

She-Aba sauntered up to the closest guard, who must have towered over her by three heads, even with her new shoes on. She inspected his skin. "You sure could use one of my special body treatments."

Bus-Lu cackled, sounding more like an old crone than a man. "Altantis's finest officers from the bird-serpent war brought back from the dead. They are now Belial's personal temple guards."

"Belial flirts with dark vibrations, Bus-Lu," Shu-Tu replied, wrinkling her nose. "To practice necromancy is to go against the sacred laws of nature."

"Eww, you mean this soldier is…is really dead?" She-Aba asked, backing away. She tripped up and plunged backward.

104

Sharon Ledwith

Lilith and Tau were there to catch her before she hit bottom. Tau snorted. "I told you these shoes were not sensible when you traded that boat merchant for them."

"They called to me," She-Aba said haughtily. "I came. I saw. I needed. Plus they look stunning."

Lilith rolled her eyes. "Stunning, yes. Practical, no."

"These soldiers have had no life in them for a long time," Shu-Tu said, waving her hand in front of an empty face. Lilith heard one of the imprisoned snakes on his arm hiss and strike at Shu-Tu. She moved with ease, and stepped away. "Dark serpent magic is not something to be trifled with."

"Neither am I."

Lilith looked around the soulless soldiers. Belial skulked toward them from the shadows of the tiled temple compound. Now dressed in a shimmering black robe with a sash decorated with large pieces of obsidian, Belial waved the guards aside. They obeyed him instantly. A woman, with hair as red as She-Aba's, walked by his side, clinging possessively to his left arm. Lilith frowned. There was something eerily familiar about this woman, whose clear turquoise eyes washed over them like an unforgiving deluge. A deep purple gown draped her body as if she were hiding a guarded secret, and a thin gold cord with crystal embellished ends wrapped tightly around her tiny waist. Then, Lilith spotted the same leather satchel that Mica had carried hanging over this woman's left shoulder. Lilith set her jaw.

"What are you doing with that satchel?" Lilith pointed a finger at the familiar red serpent etched on the satchel.

"You are in no position to ask anything—Lilith—is it?" the red-headed woman said scowling.

"How...how does Zurumu know your name?" Ajax-ol asked in astonishment.

Tau snorted. "Mica must have told her. She's got his satchel."

"And let me add, it doesn't do a thing for your outfit." She-Aba snapped her fingers. "I would have gone with a yellow satchel and matching shoes. But that's just me."

Zurumu clicked her tongue. "The red-haired one is fiery. She-Aba, I believe? Nice shoes."

She-Aba blinked, then grinned. "Thanks, I got them for a few coins and—"

"Fire-head!" Tau yelled. "Whose side are you on?"

105

"Oh, and you must be Tau," Zurumu said, sashaying away from Belial's side. "I thought I smelled goat dung."

"As charming as ever, I see, Zurumu," Ajax-ol spat.

"You do not disrespect a high priestess!" Bus-Lu smacked Ajax-ol's shins with the staff. "On your knees!"

Ajax-ol winced and fell to his knees. Lilith heard Rhea gasp.

"You are correct, Zurumu," Belial said, creeping up behind her. His shadow covered Ajax-ol. "He would make a fine sacrifice to appease the disruptive vibrations these children have brought here. And, of course, to compensate for what he has done to your reputation."

Ajax-ol hung his head. "Do what you will with me. Release me of my fate. I no longer wish to be a puppet."

Zurumu grabbed Ajax-ol's chin and forced him to look at her. "We would have made a fine couple, Ajax-ol. The people of Atlantis respect the House of Ajxor. They would see our marriage as a good omen."

The muscles in Ajax-ol's neck tensed. "I would never love you the way I love—" he stopped and looked at Rhea. He averted his eyes instantly.

"I'm sorry I didn't quite catch that, Ajax-ol, the way you love who?" Zurumu said, peering around her shoulder. "That young seer—Rhea? You know that's impossible. Belial has forbidden the seers to marry."

"Leave her out of this!" Ajax-ol seethed, standing. He gripped Zurumu's shoulders, making her wince. "You betrayed my confidence. Don't deny it. We both had other plans!"

"Playtime is over," Belial said, motioning to one of his undead soldiers. "It's time to receive the consequences for your actions, Ajax-ol. To go against the king's wishes is to go against mine!"

The entropic soldier struck the back of Ajax-ol's head with the end of his spear. He released Zurumu and plummeted to his knees. "Ajax-ol!" Rhea screamed. She sprinted toward him, but Shu-Tu grabbed her arm and pulled her back.

"Leave this to Poseidon, Rhea," Shu-Tu said sternly. "Know when to act, and when to think."

Bus-Lu leaned against the gold staff and snickered. Tau's life seal—still attached to the staff—jiggled with his sickening vibrations. "I swear you're getting wiser with age, Shu-Tu."

Sharon Ledwith

Belial bent down, grabbed Ajax-ol's hair, and pulled his head back. "After I deal with the children, I will personally see to it that your eyes never wander again by burning them out of your sockets. You will marry Zurumu, and you will fulfill the contract between Atlantis and the House of Ajxor."

"But...but what of the sacrifice?" Zurumu asked, her voice catching in her throat. Lilith noticed she gripped the strap of the leather satchel tightly.

"I've had a change of heart, Zurumu. You are to be rewarded for your insight. This marriage is your reward." Belial stood, the cords in his neck pinched as he glared at her. "Is there a problem with my decision?"

Zurumu's face tightened. "No, Belial. Your will be done." She loosened her grip on the satchel, placed her hands together, and bowed.

"Shall I have the guards bring up the seer's tusked beast for your sacrifice, Belial?" Bus-Lu asked, bowing too. He stole a look at Shu-Tu and sneered.

"That won't be necessary, Bus-Lu," Belial said, swishing his spindly fingers. "I have a better sacrifice in mind." His eyes swept over Lilith, She-Aba, and Tau. "A much better one."

"Belial," Shu-Tu said in a respectful tone, stepping closer to him. "What if these children are part of the prophecy? Surely you cannot go against what is meant to be?"

"Yeah, you don't want to do something to us that you'll regret," She-Aba said, wagging a finger.

Belial's upper lip quivered. "I already regret not beheading you in the courtyard."

Tau snorted. "You make me proud that I'm from the Black Land." He pounded his chest, making his Babel shake. "You call us savages, but you're the real savage!"

Belial bowed. "Thank you for volunteering to be the first sacrifice." He pointed to the closest lifeless soldier. "Take him to the second tier and chain him to the sacrificial pillar."

Lilith's mouth went dry. She quickly scanned the temple. Sickly smells of strong incense almost made her gag. Strange, pungent flowers hung from the walls, drooping and silently pleading for water. Huge, potted plants with leaves that fanned out as wide as Elie's body were placed strategically in front of each of the temple columns. A tall, shimmering quartz crystal cluster, the likes Lilith

107

Legend of the Timekeepers

had never seen before, was set in the middle of the compound on a pedestal of orichalcum, gold, and silver. *Where is he, where is he*, her mind buzzed, her eyes darted around. A movement from behind a golden statue of Elem, the reigning king of Atlantis, caught her off guard. She squinted and then smirked.

"The prophecy," Lilith said loudly. She put a finger on each temple. "It flows through me, speaks to me. This is not good. I see darkness, fire, and destruction here."

"What are you playing at, Lilith?" Zurumu asked through clenched teeth.

"Mica—the one who came before us—cannot be trusted. He wears a life seal imprinted with serpents and spirals. He is the one you should be afraid of. He brought you that satchel at a great price to Atlantis."

"Do not listen to her, Zurumu!" Mica shouted, coming out from behind King Elem's statue. "She doesn't know I do this to save Atlantis, not destroy it."

Mica's pale green attire looked rumpled. Lilith spotted the crystal trident he had taken from the keystone in the seventh Arch of Atlantis stuffed in his sash, next to his snake-charming flute. His face looked haggard, his sun-hued hair disheveled, but his green eyes were alert.

Lilith's stomach churned, her skin prickled. She balled her fists as tight as she could and stamped her foot. "You…you coward! Why would you use your cobra against my father? He's done nothing to you! He could be dead because of you!"

Mica held up his hands. "All will be well, I assure you, Lilith. I sacrifice much so that Atlantis will thrive."

"And now Tau's about to be sacrificed! Y-You're nothing but a backstabbing, poisonous serqet!" Lilith seethed.

"Hey, you just pronounced serqet properly," She-Aba said.

"Yes," Tau said, nodding. "Lilith's not an Atcha anymore, she's one of us."

Tears welled in Lilith's eyes. "I'd…I'd rather be from the Black Land than from Atlantis. There's too much darkness here."

"Lilith, you must understand." Mica walked closer to her. "If I fix things, then maybe we could be more than just friends…someday."

108

"F-Fix things?" Lilith roughly wiped her eyes. "You can't fix things! Our history is written, our history is done! To do so would go against the law of circular motion!"

Mica shrugged. "Laws can change."

"Not sacred laws, Mica," Shu-Tu spoke up. "Those laws separate cosmos from chaos."

"I...I trusted you! You were my friend!" Tau yelled, lunging at Mica. One of Belial's soldiers reached out and grabbed Tau by the throat. The soldier raised him off the ground. Tau's legs flailed like a fish on a hook.

"Enough of this childish banter!" Belial roared. "Take this insignificant bug to the second tier, now!"

A sudden rumble shook the compound. Statues teetered, then stilled. "You anger Poseidon, Belial," Shu-Tu warned, pointing at him. "You go against one of the most important of the sacred laws. Nothing must be done to harm the children, for eternal life comes through children."

Belial's face darkened. "These sacred laws need rewriting, Shu-Tu. They are outdated and of no use to me." He turned to Bus-Lu. "Escort the seers to the second tier so they can witness firsthand what I think about not harming the children!"

"No, wait!" Mica yelled. "This...this wasn't supposed to happen. Istulo promised me—"

"Istulo?" Lilith cut in. "What does she have to do with this?"

"Istulo assigned this important task to me," Mica replied, raking his hair.

"But, Istulo told us you wanted revenge and would do whatever it took to change your future," Lilith said.

Mica's face hardened. "No. That wasn't her plan."

"You mean this was all planned by Istulo?" She-Aba asked, rocking back and forth on her feet, as if her shoes were suddenly uncomfortable. "You being here? Us being here?"

"Only me," Mica replied, shaking his head. "I was to deliver the satchel to a high priestess Istulo had once revered named Zurumu in the Temple of Poseidon and then return home through the seventh Arch of Atlantis. That's why I took the crystal trident. Istulo promised me a different life if I accepted this task. My parents would survive. I wouldn't be alone."

"Y-You w-were n-n-never a-a-alone, m-monkey-b-butt!" Tau seethed, holding onto the undead soldier's hand, while dangling in

Legend of the Timekeepers

mid-air. "I-I w-was y-your fr-friend! M-My f-f-family w-was y-your f-f-family!"

Lilith clasped her hands together. "So what's in the satchel that you think is more important than my father's or Tau's life?"

Mica stared at the polished tile floor. "A book. Istulo calls it the Book of Mysteries. She says it is the knowledge of all that is."

She-Aba gasped. "But…but I thought the Book of Mysteries was just a rumor floating around the temples and market places. Most of the high-ranking officials say that too much power exists in that book, and no one should possess it."

"Do you know what you've done, Mica?" Lilith asked, shaking her head. "You've changed everything! You've disrupted the natural laws by bringing imbalance here! I…I hate you!"

"How touching," Belial said sneering. "However, we have a sacrifice to get to."

"No, take me instead," Mica said, standing in front of the undead soldier holding Tau. "I submit myself."

Another tremor shook the ground. Belial looked up past the open compound and into the sky. Lilith gazed up too. Behind the Temple of Poseidon loomed Mount Atlas, the active volcano providing both creation and destruction throughout Atlantis's history. Dark plumes of smoke billowed from its open mouth, followed by sickly green gases.

Belial nodded. "Very well. You'll go first. The mouthy one will go second."

"That wasn't the bargain!" Mica balled his fists. "Take me and let him go!"

Belial twisted to face Mica. His glimmering black robe spiraled around his thin legs. "I. Don't. Bargain. Captains of Atlantis, bring the children to the second tier. The volcano gods will have atonement! And I will have peace!"

Zurumu started to back away, her hand covering the satchel. Belial twirled and grabbed her wrist. "Not so fast, you have an obligation to fulfill."

"I…I was going to prepare for my marriage vows," Zurumu replied.

Belial waved his hand. "You look beautiful as you are. What you're wearing will do." Then he sneered. "Besides, the groom won't be able to see what you are wearing anyway."

Zurumu curtly nodded. "If that is your wish, Belial."

"I have another." Belial let go of her wrist and held out his hand. Orichalcum rings with dark crystals adorned his fingers. "Give me the Book of Mysteries."

She raised her dimpled chin. "It...it was given to me, as a gift."

Lilith unclasped her hands. Her nostrils flared. The burning incense was dissipating enough for her to catch a whiff of Zurumu's strong perfume. It was overpowering to the point of sickening. Zurumu gripped the strap on the satchel so tight her knuckles turned white. Cautiously, she stepped back, opened the satchel, and pulled out a pressed papyrus book as thick as three of Lilith's stacked fingers, bound with coiled strips of orichalcum. The front cover glittered with gems and stones and pearls. Embedded in the middle of the cover sat a heart-shaped crystal the size of a fig. The title was written in Atlantean geometric symbols from ancient times.

Suddenly, a strong wind picked up, blowing the potted plants around. A rumble lasting only a breath escaped from the earth. A line of thick white smoke snaked into the tiled compound, dispersing like fingers. Lilith looked down as the smoke blanketed her feet, giving a feeling of protection. Then the smoke swirled around her legs, going up and around her body. Her nose wrinkled. The smoke smelled surprisingly fresh, like it had a life, a spirit. And it seemed more animated than Belial's necromantic soldiers.

"What's the meaning of this?" Belial growled, glaring at the ground around him.

"Smoke from the ferry you commanded to be set on fire," Shu-Tu said. Then she smiled. "It is white. An auspicious sign."

As the smoke spiraled up Lilith's body, a sense of calmness vanquished her foreboding feelings. She closed her eyes, took a deep breath, and welcomed this new presence into her mind. *Lilith, use the power of all things, dance the dance of spirals.* Startled, Lilith opened her eyes. "Etan?" she muttered.

Ajax-ol jerked. "Etan?" He stood, rubbing the back of his head. "B-But that's impossible. He died...in my arms."

"Nothing is impossible, Ajax-ol," Rhea said, standing in a spiral of smoke. "Etan whispers from behind the veil."

"He whispered to you too?" Lilith asked. "What did he say?"

Rhea smiled. "Sing. He wants me to sing."

"Then you shouldn't disappoint him," Lilith said, grinning.

Lilith started swaying and moving the moment Rhea's enchanting voice resounded. The pitch, intensity, and timbre of her

Legend of the Timekeepers

voice pierced through Lilith's skin and pulsed throughout her body at an alarming rate. As the tempo changed up, so did Lilith's actions. Joyous, blissful energy flooded her insides. Lilith imagined being in the center of a spiral, as she moved in and out, holding out her arms wide, then pulling them in, like a flower blooming one moment, then closing its petals the next. The white smoke imitated her actions swirling around her, then moving outward to She-Aba, then Tau, then Mica, and returning to her. *Power in, power out, power in, power out,* she thought. This feeling was delicious to her, and with each rotation she gained more awareness.

The undead soldier holding Tau shuddered and dropped him. Cringing in distress, all of Belial's soldiers covered their ears and dropped to their knees. The snakes bound on their arms hissed and slithered back and forth, attacking the air and then themselves. The soldier's leathery skin rippled and rolled like waves in a storm in response to the musical tones until their bodies started breaking apart like land during the throes of an earthquake. Flies and gnats spewed out their mouths, noses, and ears, until all the soldiers transformed into a pile of dust on the tiles.

"Sons of Belial!" Belial screeched. "I command you to kill the singer and the dancer!"

Armed Black Priests charged from both sides of the temple, storming the compound. Some had orichalcum spears while others had golden swords or bejeweled daggers. Lilith continued with her spiral dance, the smoke circling around her, in and out, in and out. She visualized herself as part of the sun, of the stars, and beyond, then returned here as part of the earth, of her body, and all of nature.

Suddenly, all the potted plants in the compound responded to the spiral energy Lilith was generating by swaying their huge leaves back and forth, tripping many of the priests, and slowing them down. Rhea continued singing, reaching heights in her voice such as Lilith had never heard before. The gigantic crystal cluster in the middle of the temple's compound started to gyrate and vibrate to Rhea's unique pitch. In that moment, Rhea opened her arms wide, took a deep breath, and threw her head back. Lilith frowned. She didn't hear anything.

The crystal cluster shattered, sending out shards toward the assaulting Black Priests. Screams ripped through the temple, many of the priests crumbled to the floor, blinded by the sharp pieces. Other priests were not so lucky with large crystals sticking out of their chests. A flying crystal fragment came close to hitting Lilith before it exploded into a light mist. Two crystal shards whizzed toward Tau and Mica, both shards evaporating within a few strides of the boys. She-Aba covered her head and ducked only to get sprinkled with a fine spray. Before Ajax-ol and Rhea were pelted by soaring sharp crystals, the shards vibrated and burst into a fine drizzle. Shu-Tu and the seers stood calmly while crystal pieces vaporized all around them. Even Belial, Bus-Lu, and Zurumu escaped the fate of the Black Priests as crystals dissolved in mid-air before reaching them. Lilith felt her body slowing down, her mind swimming in the flow, and her heart beating in a different, stronger way. Her face slick with sweat, she stumbled. Mica caught her before she fell. Their eyes locked, and he squeezed her arm gently.

The smoke dissipated, furling like newborn ferns as it changed to gauzy, then glassy, until the air was clear around them. Belial snarled. "What manner of magic is this?"

"Not magic, Belial," Shu-Tu replied. "Power. Personal power."

Rhea screamed, breaking the bond between Lilith and Mica. Bus-Lu laughed wickedly, Ajax-ol's staff pressed into Rhea's neck to silence her beautiful voice. He dragged Rhea toward the steps of the temple's second tier, kicked away crystal pieces that littered his path, and maneuvered around the dead bodies of fallen priests. "Belial, you will have your sacrifice!"

"Nooo!" Ajax-ol yelled, picking up an orichalcum spear next to a pile of dust. He raced after Bus-Lu.

Zurumu laughed. "I told you not to trust Lilith, Belial. But you didn't listen. You never listen to your most loyal followers." She cracked open the Book of Mysteries. "And now, it's time that you listen to me."

"I don't like the way this is going," She-Aba muttered.

Tau nodded. "For once, we're in agreement."

Belial glared at the red-headed high priestess. "You dare to defy me, Zurumu?"

"It's time for a change of command, Belial," she said holding her chin high. "And I nominate myself."

Zurumu dipped into the satchel and pulled out a ceramic vial. She tore off the wax seal with her teeth and drank what was in it in one gulp. Pitching the vial at Belial's feet, she smirked, gazed down into the book Mica had delivered to her, and began to recite from it.

Legend of the Timekeepers

"What kind of language is that?" She-Aba asked, backing away to stand next to Lilith and Mica.

"I...I don't know, I've never heard that dialect before," Lilith said. "Can't you or Tau understand what she's saying through your Babel necklaces?"

"I can't," Tau said, shrugging. "It sounds like she's talking with a mouthful of long yellow fruit to me."

"It is the language of the shadows," Shu-Tu said. "It is forbidden to speak it."

Lilith swallowed hard and looked over her shoulder. Bus-Lu had managed to drag Rhea up to the first marble stair. Ajax-ol chased after them, screaming Atlantean obscenities at Bus-Lu. Lilith's ears grew hot.

Zurumu stopped reciting. She closed the book and slipped it into the satchel. She raised her arms and clapped nine times while spinning around, moving against the sun's direction instead of with it. Then she stopped and looked down at her feet. She frowned. Slowly, she placed her hands on her forehead, her nose, her lips, her chin, her throat, and her chest. Her breathing hastened, and her face flashed red.

Belial laughed. "Is that supposed to impress me?"

"Looks like she's going through the same changes my mother is," She-Aba whispered.

Zurumu glared at Mica. "He...he tricked me, Belial!" she seethed, pointing. "He made me turn against you!"

"I don't see any dagger at your throat, Zurumu," Belial replied, his lips curling up. "However, I do believe I smell the stench of betrayal."

"That's kind of like the jar calling the urn black," Tau muttered.

She-Aba stifled a giggle the same moment a strong tremor shot through the ground and knocked them all off their feet. Statues rocked, potted plants rolled onto their sides, hanging flowers trembled, and the crystal shards on the tiles amplified the sound of the earth's displeasure. As Bus-Lu lugged Rhea up the marble stairs, the tremor intensified, splitting the staircase open. A wide slithering fissure tore through the second tier of the temple.

Bus-Lu swung Rhea around to shield himself from Ajax-ol. She flailed and kicked, trying to scream, but it was useless. Bus-Lu held Ajax-ol's staff firmly across her throat, pulling it in tighter as Ajax-ol approached. Ajax-ol froze, tossed the spear aside, and put up his

114

Sharon Ledwith

arms in stalemate. Bus-Lu cackled like a crow, as he pulled Rhea up to the next step.

"This must be it," Lilith said, licking her dry bottom lip. "The beginning of the first major quake. It will come in three terrible earth shakes."

"So did we do it?" She-Aba asked, looking around.

Mica frowned. "Do what?"

"Return the One who must banish evil," Tau replied, standing and spreading his legs wide.

"What are you talking about?" Mica asked, jumping up to help Lilith and She-Aba to their feet.

"The Children of the Law of One gave us a task. A task that they scribed through Tau," Lilith said, trying to seek balance with the shaking earth. "We were pulled into the Arch of Atlantis after you went through. We...we thought since you were never supposed to be here, you were the evil to be banished."

Mica hung his head. "I...I can see why you would think that. I'm...I'm so sorry. I believed in Istulo."

Tau clipped him across the back of the head. "You should believe in yourself first! That's what my parents always tell us!"

"Now that's the smartest thing I've heard come out of your mouth, bug-boy," She-Aba said with both arms out, trying to balance on her high heels.

Suddenly, screams of pain and horror were heard coming from outside of the temple. The earthquake's intensity lessened enough to keep them from toppling over. Weakened decorated pieces of columns in the temple broke away and crashed onto the tiles. Shu-Tu managed to crawl over to Lilith and grabbed her foot. Her eyes were going back and forth at such a velocity Lilith had a hard time focusing on her face. Mica grasped the back of Shu-Tu's elbows and gently pulled up the seer.

"Atlantis...portions of our land, breaking apart, sinking fast," she said quickly. "I see this, I know this."

Lilith gulped. "Soon, the southwestern part of Atlantis will be gone forever."

Shu-Tu's eyes crossed. "Belial's kingdom grows smaller."

"You mean my kingdom, ssseer!" Zurumu hissed.

Lilith's eyes widened. Something sounded terribly wrong with the high priestess's voice. Low, constricted, reptilian. Like the sound of a human-snake hybrid. A sudden shriek resounded from

Legend of the Timekeepers

Zurumu. Her whole body vibrated and writhed across the floor. Her skin hardened, then blistered, then wept until it changed into a combination of green scales and sickly skin. Her legs rippled and entwined, transforming into a long, serpentine tail. Then Zurumu's face elongated, her nose and eyes pulled away from her skull, and a cobra's hood flared out the back of her head. Fangs grew from her open mouth, and a forked tongue flickered. Her arms shrunk to half their size, and without any shoulders, the satchel containing the Book of Mysteries slid off her arm, dropping to the trembling tiles. Lilith shuddered. The only thing that remained human was Zurumu's thick, red hair.

Belial lunged for one of his disintegrated soldier's orichalcum spears and held it up. "Kill the children and seers, and I will consider sharing my secrets with you, Zurumu."

Zurumu released a giant hiss. "I thought you didn't bargain, Belial?"

Belial's face twitched. "I don't. This is a one-time offer."

"I don't need you!" She revealed her fangs and struck at Belial.

In the blink of an eye, he disappeared in a cloud of smoke only to reappear behind her. Belial jabbed her hood with the spear. Zurumu twisted and hissed, her long tail pulling the satchel closer. "I believe you do," Belial said mockingly.

As the ground rumbled, Zurumu snapped at Belial again, only to receive the same outcome. He vanished, materialized behind her, and stabbed her again, this time with more force. "I can do this all day, Zurumu, can you?"

Her reptilian nostrils flared, and she flicked her forked tongue. "Very well, I wisssh to rule by your ssside."

"Do as I bid, and then we'll talk, Zurumu," Belial sneered. He pointed at Lilith. "Take care of the spiral dancer first."

She nodded sharply. The end of her tail wrapped around the satchel's strap and held it tight. Then she let out a monstrous hiss and slithered toward Lilith. Tau rolled across the tiles to pick up the closest discarded orichalcum spear. Zurumu snapped at him before he had time to attack and yanked away the spear, leaving him at the mercy of her wicked whims.

"Tau!" Mica threw him his flute. "Play your heart out!"

Tau snatched the flute in mid-air. He screeched out a tune, sounding like a cat with its tail caught in a chariot's wheel. Zurumu threw back her hooded head and hissed. Her arms were too short to cover her ears, so she twitched and writhed, and crawled away from him.

"That's music to my ears," She-Aba said, clapping.

Suddenly, Zurumu's tail whipped around. With the satchel still in her possession, she whacked Tau across the head with it and sent him flying over the quaking compound. Mica's flute smashed against a statue and broke in two. She hissed in victory, then turned on Lilith and spit a venomous stream at her. Lilith twirled around and ducked. The venom hit a marble post next to her. Lilith's chest tightened, watching the poison bubble and foam, devouring the marble, and weakening the post enough for it to crumble. Some of the poison dripped onto scattered crystal shards, but instead of dissolving like the marble, the crystals neutralized the venom and turned black where the venom had landed. An Atlantean principle her mother had taught her stirred Lilith's memory. *The human body is like liquid crystal. This is why crystals have such great power to affect our bodies and our souls.* She reached for the longest, sharpest, most pure shard.

Fight fire with fire, Etan whispered, as soon as Lilith touched the crystal. His voice instantly calmed her. Even with all the rumbling and tremors and screaming going on around her, Lilith took a deep breath, stood up, and turned to face her biggest fear. Knowing she needed to get closer to Zurumu, Lilith exhaled and did the only thing she could think of to charm a snake. She took a few steps forward and began to rapidly move her hands around in the air like Mica had done with Kheti. "You are nothing but a weak, pathetic, poisonous woman, Zurumu!"

"Is that ssso?" Zurumu hissed, moving her head back and forth in an attempt to focus on her.

"It is," Lilith said, now bobbing her body up and down, and waved her hands faster. "And you know what else, snake-face?" *Come on, that's it, just a little closer.*

Zurumu's reptilian eyes narrowed. "Do tell."

Lilith was within three strides of the transformed high priestess. She stopped bobbing and weaving long enough to yell, "You make me feel ashamed of my Atlantean roots!"

"Then allow me put you out of your misssery!" Zurumu lunged at Lilith.

Legend of the Timekeepers

Ducking, Lilith squeezed the crystal, then plunged it into Zurumu. She rolled far enough away from Zurumu's coils to stand and yell, "Poison in, poison out!"

The crystal shard pierced the base of Zurumu's scaly throat. Her screaming hiss rivaled the earth's relentless rumblings. Small, reptilian arms scrambled to yank the shard out, and she pitched it across the trembling tiles. Gasping for breath and clutching her bleeding throat, she bent her body forward, as if trying to catch something precious. She shuddered once, twice, thrice, before her face started to vibrate and transform back into her human features. Strangely, her cobra's hood and serpent body remained intact and unchanged.

Shu-Tu picked up the crystal. She smiled wryly and held up the crystal shard to show Lilith. The once white crystal had changed to the darkest black. "Too pure for Zurumu to handle, I see."

The red-headed cobra unfurled her hood, rolled onto her coils, and charged at Lilith. Mica jumped her from behind. He wrapped his legs around her scaly torso, held onto her red hair with a hand, and pulled the crystal trident from his sash with his other hand. He plunged the trident deep into the back of her neck. Her turquoise eyes widened in disbelief, and she released a primal scream, sounding more animal than human. She balked and threw off Mica just before going into convulsions.

"And this is for Tau!" She-Aba stabbed the high heel of her shoe into the end of Zurumu's tail. She flinched, and her tail loosened its grip to release the satchel. She-Aba scooped it up and scuffled away.

"Thanks, She-Aba," Tau said, staggering up behind her, rubbing his head. "I'm getting to like your new shoes more and more."

She-Aba roped the leather satchel's strap over one shoulder, and winked at him. "There's hope for you yet."

The earth suddenly ceased trembling and shaking, but Zurumu continued to tremor. Holding her chest, she wriggled and writhed until her tail forked to a pair of shapely human legs and her cobra's hood shriveled into oblivion. Then Zurumu's arms lengthened and green scales changed to pale skin leaving her exposed and helpless like a newborn baby. With a shaking hand, she reached over her head and wrenched the crystal trident out of the back of her neck.

"Oh…my…Ra! The crystal trident…it turned black!" She-Aba yelled.

"W-Will that still work to get us home?" Tau asked.

118

Sharon Ledwith

"I...I don't know," Lilith said, clasping her hands. A large, tanned hand took up both her hands and unclasped them. Mica looked down at her.

"Don't worry, Lilith. Whatever her plans, Istulo will make sure we get back," he said with assurance.

"I...I curse you all!" Zurumu seethed, pointing to Lilith, Mica, She-Aba, and Tau with the black trident. "I curse you, and your bloodlines to be trapped by the dark ages of time forever!"

"Very strong words for a high priestess who's about to be banished," Belial said, skulking up behind her. He ripped the black trident out of her hand.

"Banished? But...but we had a deal!"

"And I've had another change of heart." He sneered, wiping the black trident across Zurumu's face to remove her blood. "I don't need you. I only need your book. Now leave, before I decide to *curse* you."

Legend of the Timekeepers

12. The Point of No Return

"Give me the satchel, girl," Belial commanded, thrusting the trident's pointed end at She-Aba's throat.

She-Aba's eyes bugged. Her bottom lip quivered as she hugged the satchel to her body.

"It's all right, She-Aba. Give it to him," Lilith said, touching her shoulder. She eyed Belial, and smirked. "After all, it will come back to its rightful owner eventually."

Belial's upper lip curled. "Not where I'm taking it!" He waved the black trident in Lilith's face. "With this bewitched trident, I now have power over the arches. I've decided to leave Atlantis, and I'm using the seventh Arch of Atlantis as a portal for my means of departure."

Lilith stiffened. "But...you can't do that."

Belial's nostrils flared. "I can do whatever I wish. That's the benefit of being me."

"Why would you do this?" Shu-Tu asked, ambling up behind them. The other seers remained back a respectable distance.

"You said it yourself, Shu-Tu. There is the known and the unknown. I am the unknowable, and Atlantis obviously cannot handle the power I wield. To assure the survival of Atlantis, I must

121

Legend of the Timekeepers

leave. Besides—" Belial's nostrils flared, his eyebrows lowered and pinched "—I need a new country to rule, new blood to conquer. And the Book of Mysteries will help me get what I want."

Belial reached out to coil his hand around the satchel's strap. He wrenched it from She-Aba's shoulder. She winced, clutching her life seal brooch that secured her spotted animal skin around her shoulders. "Fine, but don't mess with the outfit."

The sound of Elie trumpeting caught Belial off guard. The white tusked beast charged into the Temple of Poseidon with Anapa sitting on her back. He kicked behind her ears, guiding her toward Ajax-ol. What was left of the chain that had imprisoned Elie to the giant tree trunk dragged behind her, broken links tinkled across the polished temple tiles with each stride. Bus-Lu shrieked, seeing the huge creature storm across the compound toward him, and he pushed Rhea into the chasm in the stairs.

"Rhea!" Ajax-ol yelled, grabbing the spear off the ground and throwing it across the open stairway.

Rhea bounced off the opposite side, her hands clambering over the stairs, trying to claw, to reach the spear before her body slid down the deep crack. With a loud gasp, Rhea pushed her body away from the ledge far enough to seize the spear and keep her safe.

Anapa led Elie to where Rhea dangled. Elie's long snout wrapped around Rhea's slim waist and pulled her up and away from the fissure. Ajax-ol's arms were around Rhea the moment Elie gently placed her on the tiles.

Bus-Lu crawled to the top of the stairs of the second tier with no sacrifice to show for his efforts. He wiped his fat face, then stood and raised the staff of Ajax-ol he had used to restrain Rhea. Bus-Lu shook the staff vigorously, screaming blasphemous words down at the embracing couple. Mount Atlas rumbled and red lava exploded from its top, causing the earth to tremor again.

Bus-Lu lost his footing and plummeted down the stairs. He released Ajax-ol's staff, trying to grasp onto a stair, and it clattered down in a straight line to land at Ajax-ol's feet. Bus-Lu slid sideways toward the chasm where he had tried to toss Rhea. The spear Ajax-ol had thrown for Rhea was still lying across, so the Black Priest reached out to grab it. Catching it with one hand, he pulled himself up enough to grasp the spear with his other hand. He laughed maniacally and swung his thick legs like a pendulum in an attempt to scale up one side. Bus-Lu missed the edge, and twisted

122

his body enough to dislodge the spear from the stairs. With nothing to hold onto, he plunged down the chasm, screaming all the way. Another quake summoned the earth to move in another direction, closing the fissure until the stairs fit together again.

"Bus-Lu was true to his word," Belial said with a hint of amusement. "I did get my sacrifice." Then he laughed and swirled his black robe around him, disappearing in a cloud of greenish smoke.

Tau coughed, covering his mouth. "Where'd that sneaky serqet go?"

"Over there," She-Aba said, waving away the smoke. She pointed toward Zurumu crawling slowly across the floor toward a side aisle of the temple.

"I said serqet, not snake, fire-head."

Lilith fanned the air. "Belial's probably going to the second tier of the temple to the Chamber of the Arches. That's where the seven Arches of Atlantis are kept. He's got the trident, so he's probably going to try to use it."

"Then that's where we're going," Mica said, grabbing her arm.

Shu-tu placed a hand on Lilith's heart before she left. "Remember, know when to act, and when to think."

"I will." Lilith placed her hand over the old seer's wrinkled hand. "Please, leave Atlantis, and go to the Black Land. You'll be safe there."

Shu-Tu pressed a finger to the middle of her forehead. Her eyes juggled around in her skull, then crossed. "I will stay here as long as I am needed." She removed her finger. "Do not worry, Lilith, the prophecy is now clear."

"We must go," Mica urged. "The earth will shake again."

Elie trumpeted. Lilith jumped, releasing Shu-Tu's hand. Ajax-ol and Rhea were hand in hand as they joined them. Anapa, still on top of Elie's back, loomed behind the couple. Ajax-ol saluted them with his decorated gold staff. Anapa climbed down, using Elie's thick, wrinkled leg for support. Tau smiled. "I thought hybrids weren't allowed in the Temple of Poseidon?"

Anapa shrugged. His gold earring flickered mischievously. "I weighed the consequences of my actions, and all was balanced. Besides, I owe a debt again to Etan. I will watch over Ajax-ol until the debt is repaid."

Legend of the Timekeepers

"We've decided to go to the Black Land," Ajax-ol announced, squeezing Rhea's hand. "Atlantis no longer feels like home."

"You wish to leave with him, Rhea?" Shu-Tu asked, though it sounded more of a blessing than a question.

Rhea placed her hands together and bowed before Shu-Tu. "It is my destiny, to be with Ajax-ol. I know this, feel this in my heart."

Shu-Tu nodded sharply. "Then follow your heart. Go, do, be, Rhea."

"Here," She-Aba said, retrieving her snake-skin satchel from underneath the spotted animal cape. She slid off her gold bracelets and rings and stuffed them in it. "You'll need this to get you all to the Black Land safely. You'll also find items inside that any sensible young seer could use."

Tau frowned. "You're giving her your make-up satchel?"

"What can I say, I'm in the giving mood," She-Aba replied, shrugging.

Rhea accepted the satchel with a bow. She peered inside it and nodded. "Your generosity will be rewarded. Know this, trust in this."

An intense tremor rolled through Lilith, signaling to her that the end of this first major quake was near. "You need to go—" She pointed to the arched entrance. "—before the bridges are no longer passable."

"We shall travel around the channels," Anapa announced. "I know of a docked barge big enough that can take us out to the ocean." He stroked Elie's long snout. "All of us."

Ajax-ol left Rhea's side and hugged Lilith fiercely. Her feet dangled for a moment before he placed her down. "I'll never forget you or your friends."

"Well, I am pretty unforgettable," She-Aba said, winking.

Tau groaned. "That's for sure. And believe me, I've tried."

"Come on, before this quake gets worse," Mica said, pulling Lilith away.

"Wait, here, Tau," Ajax-ol said, untying the life seal from his staff. "I believe this belongs to you." He placed it over Tau's head.

"Thanks, Ajax-ol," Tau said, placing his seal next to his Babel necklace. "I felt naked without this."

"Now there's a vision I'll need the healers to wash from my mind," She-Aba said, grimacing.

124

A strong, vicious jolt shook them. "You must go," Shu-Tu said, backing away and pointing to the second tier of the Temple of Poseidon. "Go. Banish evil."

Stumbling, then sprinting toward the stairs, Lilith, Mica, Tau, and She-Aba raced across the tiled compound, dodging dead bodies, fallen statues of kings and queens, and crystal shards. She-Aba's heel got caught in a gap of broken tile, and she tripped and fell. Tau skidded and went back to help her up. Her shoe was stuck, so he undid it and released her foot. She tried to yank her shoe free, but it was no use, as the ground continued to move and shake.

"Leave it, She-Aba," Lilith yelled from the bottom of the stairs. "It's just a shoe!"

Swirling her spotted animal skin around her shapely body, She-Aba pulled off her other shoe and bolted toward them. "I'll never see another pair of shoes like that in my life!"

"For Ra's sake, just make a pair!" Tau yelled in exasperation. He grabbed her arm and led her up the stairs.

At the top of the second tier, several high priests scurried around collecting priceless Atlantean artifacts and covering statues with purple cloths. Two priests wearing black robes and silver laurels were tending to a fire in the long pit at the base of the sacrificial pillar, stirring up the charred remains of a bull's skull and other unfortunate victims. The set of golden chains hanging from the pillar vibrated along with the earth's movements while the priests chanted Atlantean prayers.

Lilith quickly scanned the rest of glittering room, then spotted the most beautiful statue in the Temple of Poseidon, positioned in the center of the room. Her shoulders drooped, her chest ached. This would be the last time she'd ever lay her eyes on it again. The huge golden statue of Poseidon standing on a chariot pulled by six winged horses sparkled amongst the chaos going on all around them. Smaller statues of graceful sea nymphs riding on the backs of golden dolphins surrounded Poseidon's magnificent effigy. Walls of ivory enhanced with gold, silver, and orichalcum brightened the enormous area. Lilith's whole body tingled and she lightly touched her chest, suddenly feeling like a princess returning home.

"Which way, Lilith?" Tau asked, breathing hard.

"I think the chamber where the arches are kept is that way," Mica said, pointing toward the left. "I'm sure that's the way I came through when I was searching for Zurumu."

Legend of the Timekeepers

"Belial, I beg of you! Noooo!" a voice cut through the rumbling.

She-Aba raised a red brow. "I believe your suspicions have been confirmed, Mica."

Lilith nodded. "Just follow the sound of fear."

Lilith's eyes watered from the heavy smoke of burning incense. She led them down a corridor lined with silver and gold entwining serpents to the Chamber of the Arches of Atlantis. She hadn't been in this room since they had left Atlantis. It all seemed like a blur to her, the life she had led here. A solid gold archway with a sculpted orichalcum serpent motif over its top marked the entrance to the chamber. Diamond eyes in the serpent twinkled ominously. Mica and Tau pushed open the heavy gold-lined double doors. Lilith almost tripped over the dead body of a high priest. His bloodshot eyes were open and lifeless, and his bulging face was blue and blotchy.

"Careful." Mica clutched her elbow, and led Lilith away from the murdered priest. Then he pried the orichalcum spear away from the priest's rigid fingers.

Tau whistled. "This looks like the same room where your father keeps the seventh Arch of Atlantis at your home in the Black Land."

"Ours is an exact replica," Lilith replied, glancing around the deep bronze room.

Huge tapestries lined the walls, colorfully embroidered with stories and myths of Atlantis's origins. There were no windows to allow natural light in, so orichalcum urns filled with glimmering crystals were situated around the boundaries of the room. The smooth tiled, gold-flecked floor reflected the crystals' glow, illuminating the Chamber of the Arches in a holy, reverent way. Lilith's nose wrinkled, detecting a hint of mint and garlic wavering in the air.

"Ohh, look at those beautiful arches," She-Aba said, her eyes widening. "They're all different colors."

The earth continued to rumble as Lilith gazed upon the fifth arch, the darkest in color. Her breathing hastened. She had never seen this arch before. Belial had stolen it long before she was born. But her father had made sure that he passed along its teachings to her and shared what the Children of the Law of One had scribed into its magnificent columns. She remembered that the true essence of the fifth Arch of Atlantis was to help all Atlanteans acknowledge their shadow side in order to help them grow and evolve and move

126

forward with purpose. Lilith focused on the crystal trident in its keystone. The trident hummed quietly, absorbing the ethereal energy of the room. Seven spirals were engraved around the crystal trident, and underneath it, the four small, slightly slanted ancient glyphs were inscribed on every one of the arches. *Time flows through us,* she read. The same words her father shared with her before they were sucked into the seventh arch.

Lilith searched for the seventh Arch of Atlantis and found it positioned in the middle of the room at the very back, standing in front of the Creation tapestry. The arches were arranged in a semicircle with the first, third, and fifth arches to the left of the seventh arch, and the second, fourth, and sixth arches to the right. Each arch stood as high as a tusked beast, with the archway measuring at least half a tusk beast's height at the widest point. The arches were separated by a distance of at least five strides. Lilith knitted her fair brows. The keystone of the seventh Arch of Atlantis was missing its crystal trident. Sadly, the arch appeared dull, lackluster, as if the light inside had been dimmed. Lilith covered her mouth. *Thank Poseidon, it's still here!* She rushed over to it.

"Where's serqet-breath?" Tau huffed, following her.

"He's in here somewhere," Mica said, holding the spear vigilantly, looking around.

Tau snorted. "Maybe we should follow the scent of beetle dung."

"Don't insult the beetles, bug-boy, they're sacred," She-Aba said, checking out a tapestry. "This is absolutely stunning work. I must use this technique in my next—"

The whole tapestry rippled and suddenly attacked She-Aba, the corner piece rolling up and engulfing her like a burial shroud. She dropped her high-heel shoe before it wrapped around her body, leaving the bottom portion of her legs exposed. She-Aba slapped her bare feet against the white marble floor in rapid succession, struggling against the material. She thrashed, trying to say something, anything, but her screams were muffled.

"She-Aba!" Lilith yelled, turning away from the seventh Arch of Atlantis.

By the way She-Aba flailed and kicked, Lilith knew her breathing had been compromised enough that soon She-Aba would be out of precious air. Mica lunged at the tapestry, slicing it from the wall. He tried to rip the richly embroidered cloth away from her face with the tip of the spear. Tau was on She-Aba's other side, yanking

127

Legend of the Timekeepers

at the tapestry, but only getting a fistful of shredded threads for his effort. The tapestry squeezed around her face like the coils of a snake smothering her. Both Tau and Mica backed off while She-Aba squirmed and squirmed, smacking her feet harder. Another tremor shook the temple.

Lilith clenched her teeth and stamped her foot. "Belial! Stop this, or I swear to Poseidon I'll—"

"You'll what?" a voice cut in from a low-lit corner.

Lilith twisted around and glared at the dark magus. Belial snickered, skulking over to stand before her, his shadow swallowing any light she stood in. The smell of mint and garlic overpowered Lilith's senses, and she felt a sudden drop in pressure in the room as if an invisible shield guarding her had been ripped away. Lilith's eyes widened. Belial used the mint-garlic concoction as a way of distraction, to subdue his adversaries. Her skin tingled. He was feeding off her body's energy, pulling her personal power away from her like an inverted spiral. She needed to sever this destructive connection, dam the flow of energy between them. And there was only one way to do that. She instantly relaxed, released the tension in her jaw, and took a step forward. He fed on fear. That was evident. She inhaled in and out, in and out. *Time to give Belial indigestion.*

Lilith blocked out She-Aba's thrashing and concentrated all her attention on Belial. He gripped the black trident in his hand as if it were part of him, and the leather satchel he'd taken from She-Aba was roped over his shoulder. In her mind, she turned over what she knew of him. Belial manipulated people using fear as the foundation to get what he desired. And he was good at it. He disregarded the sacred laws, crushed spirits, and bent the people's will to his own evil ways. He cared for no one but himself. Tau was correct. Belial's true nature was aligned with a serqet's—he poisoned anyone and anything that got in his way. The hairs on the back of Lilith's neck tingled. Something didn't make sense. Belial hadn't left yet. Then it occurred to her. *Maybe he can't leave?*

"Why are you still here, Belial?"

His lips thinned. "What are you getting at?"

"You can't leave, can you? You don't know what to do." Lilith smirked. "How does it feel to feel powerless, Belial?"

His face twitched. His onyx eyes narrowed to slits.

"Spare She-Aba's life and I'll help you," Lilith offered.

"I don't make bargains!" he snapped.

The earth shook with enough force to produce cracks in the bronze ceiling. The one thing Lilith had over Belial was that she knew Atlantis would be around for another hundred years. At least part of it would be. He didn't. She also knew the southwestern portion of Atlantis was beginning its descent into the ocean and would take one-third of the population with its demise. Atlantis never truly recovered from this devastation, leaving children like Lilith and Mica to be born into an unstable and unbalanced environment. She deliberately toyed with her snake bracelet. Then she yawned.

"Fine. Go down with Atlantis," Lilith said, shrugging. "Being a Timekeeper, and knowing how to use the power of spirals, has its rewards. Besides, it won't be long before you perish along with the rest of the *ordinary* Atlanteans."

Belial growled. He snapped his fingers, causing the tapestry to go limp. Mica and Tau quickly freed She-Aba before Belial had second thoughts. Lilith peered over her shoulder. She-Aba's face was redder than her hair as she inhaled long, deep breaths like she was gulping down excess amounts of water. She checked over her face and throat, then mouthed "thank you" to Lilith. Satisfied She-Aba was safe, Lilith turned back to face the most feared man in Atlantean history.

Belial pressed the black trident's prongs into her throat. Lilith jumped. He applied pressure. "I believe it's your turn, *Timekeeper*. Show me how this works."

Remember, show him no fear. Lilith pointed to the dark trident. "Do you mind?"

Lilith had absolutely no idea how to use any of the arches as a portal. It had been pure chance or fate or destiny when the Children of the Law of One summoned the three of them through seventh Arch of Atlantis. She swallowed hard as Belial slowly removed the trident from her throat, wishing for Etan to whisper in her ear one last time. Her seer's snake bracelet slid down her forearm to imprison her wrist. She wished Shu-Tu was here with her to give her strength, to lend her voice. *Go. Banish evil.* Those were the last words Shu-Tu spoke to her. Then Lilith's eyes widened. She understood the riddle. *I'm the One who must banish evil. I'm the One who must keep time safe.* A hint of a smile emerged on her face. It was time to rid Atlantis of this man, this disease.

Legend of the Timekeepers

"You're doing it all wrong," Lilith said with a tone of authority, swishing her hand. "You need to stand in front of the arch that is the closest match to your frequency to absorb its total power."

"Lilith? What are you doing?" Mica asked, helping She-Aba up.

"Yeah, that black serqet doesn't play fair!" Tau yelled.

"Silence!" Belial thundered, as he pulled a piece of onyx off of his sash, and threw it at Mica. The black bead hit his orichalcum spear, and the spear dissolved into ashes. "If any of you move a serpent's hair, you'll join the spear on the floor."

She-Aba gulped. "But...but serpents don't have hair."

Belial sneered. "That's the point." Then he wagged the black trident in Lilith's face. "Do go on."

Lilith licked her parched lips. "What happened when you put the black crystal trident into the keystone of the seventh Arch of Atlantis?"

"I'm not up for games!" he spat.

"Neither am I. My guess is nothing happened. You couldn't activate the arch, and since none of your sorcery works on any of the arches, you were left feeling powerless."

Belial stroked his braided beard. "What is your point?"

"The point is I am a Timekeeper. *You* are not."

Belial's face twitched. "Is that supposed to impress me, girl?"

"I should think so. You forget the most sacred law of the arches," Lilith said. She cautiously walked to the front of the fifth Arch of Atlantis and pointed at the keystone. "Time flows through us."

Belial growled, creeping up behind her. "I grow weary of this game, Timekeeper." He pounced in front of Lilith and glared down at her.

A wicked tremor shot through Lilith, throwing her into Belial. He stumbled backwards slamming against the fifth Arch of Atlantis. The black trident slipped out of his hand and slid across the gyrating floor. Lilith crawled over to claim it. Belial regained his balance enough to stand inside the archway. He smoothed out his shimmering black robe, giving Lilith enough time to scoop up the black trident and stand. Another rumble from the earth confirmed her suspicions. This was the third and final shake that would separate and sink the southwestern portion of Atlantis. Even the arches trembled in unison. The fifth Arch of Atlantis shook enough to loosen its crystal trident from the keystone.

130

Sharon Ledwith

An intense heat emanating from the black trident started to burn the inside of her hand and run up the length of her arm. Her snake bracelet glowed as if she'd stuck it in a bed of hot coals. Sweat dripped down her face and body and splattered to the floor. Despicable, cold laughter, sounding like Zurumu, invaded her mind. Somehow, the evil presence of this banished high priestess was searing into Lilith, poisoning her being, setting her on fire.

Belial laughed wickedly. "You're right! I can feel the power of this arch feeding me, rejuvenating my power!" Then he patted the leather satchel and opened it. "And with this book, no power on earth will prevent me from—" His hand swished around the inside of the satchel and pulled out a handful of make-up, scents, and brushes. "What…what trickery is this?"

"I figure you could use all the help you can get with your appearance," She-Aba replied, snapping her fingers.

"Where is the Book of Mysteries?" Belial snarled, scattering the make-up and brushes.

She-Aba smirked. "I slipped it in my snake-skin satchel and gifted it to Rhea as an early wedding present. It's probably making its way to the Black Land by now."

Belial's face darkened to the color of the fifth Arch of Atlantis. He raised his thin arms over his head and started to recite an incantation in the language of the shadows. Lilith's head pounded in agony. She had to get Zurumu out of her mind, and her skin, before the high priestess completely infected her with the evil vibrations of the black trident. Lilith stared at Belial, who was just as poisonous and evil as Zurumu, and reacted in the only way she knew would release her from the hateful feelings coursing through her body. *Fight fire with fire,* Lilith thought, as she squeezed the black trident, taking in more pain and putting all her angry thoughts and feelings into it, and charged at Belial.

"Poison out, poison in!" she screamed, thrusting the trident into the dark magus.

Stumbling, Lilith fell to her knees and coddled her burning hand to her chest. She heard a terrible shriek and looked up to find Belial still standing in the center of the fifth Arch of Atlantis with the black trident protruding out of his stomach. Wisps of dark spirals shot out of the end of the black trident's handle and circled the fifth Arch of Atlantis like an army of serpents coiling around their prey.

Legend of the Timekeepers

"Lilith!" Mica yelled. She could hear his feet slapping against the tiles to reach her, his strong, slick arms cradled and lifted her away from the fifth arch. The smell, the essence of his skin made Lilith think of the Black Land.

"I thought I commanded you not to move!" Belial hissed, fumbling for another onyx bead on his sash.

Mica glared at Belial. "I do not take orders from a coward, you weak-minded snake!"

Before Belial had a chance to use the piece of onyx on Mica, a high-heel shoe flew across the room and whacked Belial in the nose. Shocked, Belial dropped the bead, cupped his face, and fell to his knees.

"Good shot, Tau!" She-Aba cheered.

"I take back what I said," Tau replied over his shoulder, running to join Mica and Lilith. "Those are the most sensible shoes ever."

"And stunning," She-Aba added, sashaying across the tiles.

The fifth arch started to blur, moving faster with each breath. A deep boom echoed from it, making the arch sound foreign and lost. The crystal trident was propelled from its keystone, as if the fifth arch was rejecting it. Tau lunged for the crystal trident before it hit the shaking marble floor. As soon as the trident connected with his hands, the earthquake ceased completely and all rumbling stopped.

"W-What's happening to me?" Belial shrieked, standing. He gripped the black trident's handle and pulled it out of his stomach. Both the fifth Arch of Atlantis and Belial were beginning to fade.

"I think you're being banished, serqet-breath," Tau said, wagging the crystal trident at him.

Belial glared at Lilith. "Remember this, *Timekeeper*," he said, his nostrils flaring. "Nothing is ever lost, only changed. Time will flow through me too. Mark my words I promise we'll meet again, in another place, in another time."

"And you mark my words, Belial, all four of us will be ready for you when we do meet," Lilith replied, her heart now thumping in strong, direct beats. "We are connected, we are one."

Belial sneered and stuffed the black trident into his sash. He pushed his palms into the center of the arch's columns and finished reciting his incantation. The fifth Arch of Atlantis hummed and droned to the sickly rhythm of the language of the shadows and continued to vibrate at an accelerated rate until it disappeared into oblivion, leaving the seventh Arch of Atlantis in plain sight.

132

Sharon Ledwith

"Where'd serqet-breath go?" Tau asked, clutching the crystal trident to his bare chest.

"All I know is that Belial settles in a portion of the land west of Atlantis, to a place where my Uncle Kukulkan will travel one hundred years from now," Lilith said, pushing a fair tendril out of her face. "My hope is that he will find Belial and bring balance back to our earth."

"That is my hope too," Mica said, gently placing Lilith down.

Lilith pushed her bracelet away from her wrist, then realized the burning sensation in her hand had disappeared the same moment Belial had left Atlantis. She wiggled her fingers, feeling no pain, no heat.

"Bet your uncle could use all the help he can get," She-Aba said, reaching for her high-heel shoe near the area where the fifth Arch of Atlantis once stood. "Is there any chance I could send this to him?"

Tau laughed. "Why waste a perfectly good shoe, fire-head?"

Lilith giggled as she let her arm fall to her side. "Now that our task for the Children of the Law of One has been completed, there is only one thing left to do."

"And what's that?" She-Aba asked, stuffing her shoe into her spotted cape's pocket.

"Bring Mica home," Lilith said, smiling. "As my father requested."

"Sounds like a plan, Timekeeper," Mica said, winking at her. "Tau, put the crystal trident into the keystone of the seventh Arch of Atlantis. It's time to go home."

Lilith leaned against Mica's tanned, sinewy arm. "Yes, home to the Black Land."

Legend of the Timekeepers

13. The Guardian of the Sands

"*I* am most disappointed," Istulo said from the corner of the Golden Serpent room.

Lilith's head wouldn't stop spinning. They emerged from the seventh Arch of Atlantis like flying fish landing on a beach. She shook her head. Did she hear Istulo correctly? *Disappointed? With whom?*

Shaken, Lilith stood and looked up over her shoulder. The crystal trident was sitting securely in the keystone of the arch, as if it had never been touched. She closed her eyes, said a quick prayer to appease Poseidon, and thanked the Children of the Law of One for safe passage home. Then she opened her eyes and glanced around for her father. Lilith found him lying on the floor four strides away from where she'd found him earlier. He'd been dragged under the tapestry embroidered with the extensive fleet of ships leaving Atlantis in all different directions before the final destruction. His chest moved up and down, up and down with the rhythm of his breath. His eyes were shut.

"Father!" She rushed toward him.

Istulo stepped in front of Lilith. "He needs his rest."

Istulo's voice sounded hardened.

Legend of the Timekeepers

Lilith frowned. "What's wrong, Istulo? And...and why did you lie to us about Mica?"

"Lie?" Istulo shrieked. Before Lilith knew what was happening, she felt the sharp sting of a slap against her cheek.

She flinched and clutched the side of her face. Her blue eyes watered.

"Oh...my...Ra! What was that for?" She-Aba yelled, jumping to her feet. She adjusted her spotted animal cape around her shoulders.

Istulo lowered her eyes to She-Aba's feet. "I see you've lost your shoes, She-Aba. Pity. They were stunning."

She-Aba froze. She inclined her head. "How...how could you possibly know about—"

"Zurumu," Mica said, his voice catching in his throat. "Y-You're really Zurumu." His face turned ashen.

"Very astute, Mica." Istulo clapped. "The potion in the satchel you delivered to me in Atlantis not only helped transformed me into a snake-hybrid, but also acted as catalyst to slow down the aging process."

"Y-You tricked me, used me," Mica stammered. "You made me believe through the interpretation of my life seal that Lilith and I were to be mortal enemies." He grasped his life seal hanging from the thong around his neck and snapped it off. "This...this was never to be my lifetime occupation!"

"It was your choice to believe the words I fed you," Istulo said, cackling. "Live with it."

Lilith gasped. "That's why you sent Mica back through the seventh Arch of Atlantis. To find you, the younger you, so that he could bring you the Book of Mysteries."

"Yes," Istulo replied, sneering. "That book was to be my redemption. The day you came to the Temple Beautiful with Tau, I recognized you at once and knew what you were. That's when everything became clear, and I saw my chance to change the prophecy and the fate of Atlantis."

"But...how did you find the Book of Mysteries?" She-Aba asked.

"I came across the book, by accident, in a forbidden section of the Temple of Sacrifice. And as you know by now, She-Aba, there are no accidents." Istulo's upper lip curled. "Scribed inside it, I found everything that would have given me my life back. Longevity potions. Elixirs. Incantations. Spells. Charms. Rituals. Secrets. I

136

knew if I had a powerful book like that in my possession while I lived in Atlantis, I would have changed things. I would have overthrown Belial. I would have ruled Atlantis. Yet, I am still here, still unchanged."

"Atlantis still would have blown up, still would have sank into the ocean!" Lilith seethed, waving her hands in the air. "Don't you see? Belial and his self-centered evil followers created too much destruction and chaos through their black magic and terrible deeds that they ultimately sealed Atlantis's fate."

"My heart bleeds for Atlantis and those pitiful victims," Istulo replied mockingly. She tapped her sagging chest. "I was abandoned by my people. They got what they deserved."

"And I was abandoned by you!" Mica yelled, shaking his life seal at Istulo. "I...I believed in you, trusted you. But...but now I see that your heart is blacker than Belial's. You deserved the life you created!"

"And now you'll have to live with your choices, Istulo!" Tau said defiantly. "Guess that makes you a creature of nature like the serqet that stung me."

"Tau's right," Lilith said, curling her fingernails into her palms. "I let you get under my skin and poison my mind once, and I'll never let you or anyone else like you do it again!"

"And when I tell my father, who sits on the high counsel, about this," She-Aba said, wagging a finger, "you'll be submitted to the Temple of Sacrifice for observation."

Istulo's top lip curled back, revealing two yellow fangs. "I think not, She-Aba."

The high priestess raised her arms and clapped nine times while chanting in the language of the shadows. Then she tore off her robe, exposing a round, faded puncture mark at the base of her neck. White scales covered her body. Istulo heaved forward and her legs entwined to form a long serpent's tail. Both her arms shortened to half their original size. She hissed, as her facial features gyrated long enough to sculpt into a cobra's pointed face and round hood. Her beady, cold eyes glared at Lilith, then at Mica.

"Thisss moment hasss kept me from going insssane," Istulo hissed, then charged them.

Lilith stumbled back. She clutched her chest. No shoe of She-Aba's would bring this vengeful high priestess down. Lilith's life seal settled in her palm. The inside of her mouth tasted like sand. All

Legend of the Timekeepers

she could think about was how Shu-Tu's calming voice gave her strength, and how Etan's words gave her wisdom, and how the law of circular motion affected everything and everyone. *Go. Banish evil.* Lilith took a chance, yanked the life seal from her neck, and, with the force of Poseidon, hurled it at Istulo.

Mica pitched his life seal at Istulo in the same moment. "Go choke on your lies, you poisonous hag!" he yelled with renewed strength.

The two life seals intertwined in mid-air, like a pair of mating eagles dancing in the sky. Istulo snapped at Lilith and Mica's spiraling life seals and swallowed them in one bite. She let out a visceral hiss, then balked and shook her cobra head, twisting and writhing and coughing as if some madness had claimed her body. Istulo started to choke, shudder, and convulse. Her small, useless arms were too short to go into her mouth to remove the small, round life seals stuck in her throat. Gasping, Istulo's eyes clouded over and rolled toward the back of her bulbous skull. She hissed out a terrible rattle before crashing to the floor.

Istulo's forked tongue flicked through the air until it fell back into her gaping reptilian mouth. Her chest heaved, small gnarled hands clawed at the floor while Istulo desperately tried to steal a breath. The long serpent tail straightened, and then lay still. Her cobra head fell to one side as death claimed the old banished high priestess once known as Zurumu. Then, with the same forces of nature that had broken apart Atlantis, her old body trembled and vibrated and burned until all that was left of Istulo was a pile of ash on the floor and her orichalcum headband.

Tau whistled. "That's one way of getting back all that you've been giving out."

"Now Istulo's got plenty of time to go meditate on those life seals," She-Aba added.

A cough and sputter made Lilith avert her eyes from Istulo's remains on the floor toward her father, now sitting up. His golden hair was tousled, but his color had returned. She smiled and ran to him with open arms. "Father! You're healed!"

She nuzzled his beard, smelling the pungent incense lingering there. At least Istulo had not wanted him dead. She had been after Lilith and her friends all along. Lilith hugged Segund fiercely.

"W-What happened, Lilith? I don't remember anything past saying good-night to you and She-Aba."

Reluctantly, she pulled away from him and sighed. She patted down his beard and said, "It's a long story, Father. I...I wouldn't know where to begin."

Suddenly, the door to the Golden Serpent's Room swung open. Standing in the doorway was the old man Lilith had bumped into in the Temple Beautiful. His wild white hair still stuck out like he'd been in one-too-many dust storms. He stiffly walked into the room using his lavishly decorated golden walking stick for support. His deep blue robe swished and sparkled with iridescence and majesty. Behind him loomed two tall soldiers wearing gold breast plates over crisp linen tunics and an old, thin woman with long white hair. She wore a silver headband and robe—the colors of a proficient healer from the Temple of Sacrifice. On her left arm dangled a seer's orichalcum snake bracelet.

"W-W-Who are you?" She-Aba stammered.

The wizen man acknowledged her with a polite nod. "I am the one called Duo-She-Dui."

She-Aba's eyes widened. She dropped to one knee and bowed. So did Tau and Mica.

Duo-She-Dui motioned for one of the guards to pass him an old snake-skin satchel beaten by time. He reached into it and pulled out a beautiful high-heel shoe decorated with strips of orichalcum and colored gems. Lilith's eyes widened. It was an exact replica of She-Aba's shoe.

"I believe this belongs to you, She-Aba," the old man said, grinning. "You, and your friends, may call me Ajax-ol."

Sweat slithered down the length of Lilith's face while she anxiously waited for the grand unveiling of the Guardian of the Sands. Carved from a single sandstone knoll, this monument had been years in the making. Speculation circled the air as to what its purpose might be. Some people thought it protected the Great Pyramid. The priests and priestesses said it would be utilized for special burial ceremonies. Still others were convinced this great structure was to be used as a repository of ancient teachings and knowledge. Whatever the Guardian of Sands' purpose was, many craftsmen had put their backs and hearts and souls into this creation,

Legend of the Timekeepers

and now it was ready to be shared with the people of the Black Land.

"Where is she?" Lilith asked, scanning the crowd.

"Fear not, Lilith, She-Aba will be here in good time," Segund replied, adjusting the new sash She-Aba had fashioned for him. This one was made of a smooth, deep red material decorated with pearls and crystals.

"She's probably changed into many outfits by now," Lilith said, wiping her face. "I wonder which one she'll finally choose."

Segund brushed the sand from his dark blue linen robe. "It doesn't matter. Nothing she wears will compare to what you have on, my daughter." Then he winked at her and glanced over at Mica standing with Tau's extensive family.

An intense heat starting from the tips of her toes flashed through Lilith's body. By the time it reached her cheeks, Mica was on the sand wrestling with one of Tau's younger brothers. Their laughter warmed her belly in a happy way. Averting her eyes toward the veiled monstrous statue, Lilith wondered what would become of her relationship with Mica now that she had decided to enter into the Arcane Tradition, a special school of occult knowledge and magical systems. Belial's threat to Lilith and her friends had helped seal that decision for her, and she wanted to be prepared for any future meetings with the dark magus. Mica had announced that he would continue with his studies as an initiate in the Temple Beautiful as all his criminal acts against Segund, and the people of the Black Land, had been forgiven by Duo-She-Dui.

Lilith removed a foot from her sandal and dipped a toe into the cool, desert sand. It was early morning so the sand hadn't had time to heat up. A breeze snaked through from the great river to the east where the Guardian of the Sands faced. She licked her lips, tasting the saltiness. Wearing a slim-fitting pale blue gown, Lilith allowed the wind to cool her body and caress her soul. A long belt made of strung shells and pearls grazed the sand with enough force to draw mini spirals. Thank Poseidon, She-Aba had come by her home earlier to style her hair up in crystal hairpins. She had even applied a minimal amount of make-up to Lilith for this special occasion before rushing home to get ready herself. Lilith slipped her sandal back on and checked the position of the rising sun by holding up her fingers against the horizon. *Four fingers to the sun, almost time for the unveiling.*

140

"Where's fire-head?" Tau asked.

Lilith dropped her arm to her side. Her orichalcum snake bracelet slid down to confine her hand. She rolled her eyes and said, "She's probably checking her hair over one last time."

Tau grunted. "It won't matter. It will still be red."

"True, but She-Aba has proven herself worthy enough to don the color of a goddess," Mica said, walking up to them.

For this special ceremony, Mica wore a light green top and pleated schenti fastened by a snake-skin sash. His golden hair was slick with perfumed oil. He placed his hands together and bowed before Lilith's father. "How is your hand, Segund?"

"Still sore," Segund said, lightly touching it. Lilith noticed her father's hand was slightly swollen, but he had gotten stronger in the last seven days. He grunted. "I don't know how anyone would choose to be a snake charmer."

"Snake charming chose me," Mica said, grinning. "It is a skill that helped me survive the harsh days after the flood. People still needed pleasure, and I provided it for them."

"I still feel bad about having to kill Kheti," Tau said. "He was a fine cobra."

"That's okay, Tau," Mica said, reaching out to tousle Tau's short-cut hair. "I think my days of snake charming are over anyway."

Lilith giggled just as the crowd suddenly started ohhing and ahhing, then applauding and cheering.

"That must be Ajax-ol and Rhea arriving," Tau said. He adjusted his crisp linen schenti accented with splashes of blue dye and proudly straightened his life seal, now attached to his Babel necklace.

"When do you start your scribing lessons, Tau?" Segund asked.

"Tomorrow at sun up," he replied, beaming. "My father and mother have been telling all the merchants and farmers about how I will be trained to scribe stories on the walls of the Great Pyramid. Father says that Ra has conspired to make my lifetime occupation come true."

Segund smiled, showing off his pearl white teeth. "Your father is a wise man, Tau."

"Move aside, move aside," a familiar voice rose above the crowd.

Lilith perked up. "Is that She-Aba?"

Mica's jaw dropped. "Maybe she is really a goddess."

"Oh…my…Poseidon," Lilith gasped.

Tau groaned. "We're never going to hear the end of this."

A finely-crafted mahogany chair, covered in spotted and striped animal pelts, was lifted high above the crowd. A canopy of fresh palm leaves protected She-Aba from the sun as she regally sat in the chair, waving and blowing kisses at everyone. Four men, who Lilith vaguely recognized as the artists she had seen in the Temple Beautiful who had harassed She-Aba, were carrying the chair on their shoulders using polished ivory tusks embedded with crystals and jewels. Lilith covered her mouth. She-Aba was dressed in a lavish light purple gown with a silver sash. Her life seal broach was brilliantly accessorized with her Babel necklace as if a master jeweler had created it. Her red hair sparkled with white crystals, and on her feet were the shoes she'd bought in Atlantis. Lilith removed her hand. The shoes were as stunning as ever.

Following She-Aba, a white tusked beast swayed side to side as it cut a wide path. Its long snout reached for the odd piece of fruit offered by a generous vender. Elaborate gold and silver ribbons were entwined around its tusks. The beast carried two older citizens who sat on their blanketed high perch waving at the cheering throng. Flanked by an elite squad of soldiers with spears and shields, the tusked beast stopped, raised its snout, and bellowed.

"Duo-She-Dui! May Ra bless you!" the people shouted.

"May Ra protect you, Mu-Elden, healer of many!" a group of women dressed in plain white sheaths screamed.

Lilith felt a light touch upon her cheek. "I must go speak with the master builder of the Great Pyramid to make preparations to move the seventh Arch of Atlantis to a more secluded area inside the pyramid," Segund said.

Lilith arched a fair brow. "Move the arch? Why, Father?"

"It will be safer for the people this way," Segund replied, sighing. "And it will keep time safe."

"I will see Lilith home, Segund," Mica said, bowing. "You have my word."

Segund grinned mischievously. "And I'll have you bound in mummy's bandages if you don't get my daughter home before our evening meal."

Mica coughed. His face reddened, and he answered Segund with a silent nod.

Sharon Ledwith

Segund winked at Lilith, then turned and trudged through the sand toward the Great Pyramid, passing a row of lit torches. Smoke from the torches carried the essence of fragrant oils. Lilith clasped her hands and inhaled deeply. Ajax-ol and Rhea had made it to the Black Land safely and changed their names to begin a new life together. The Book of Mysteries had helped them both find their purpose and build an empire, using the knowledge scribed within it for good, instead of the evil Istulo had intended. Not only had they achieved their dreams, but the dreams of others had been realized. Temples and buildings were built to teach and educate the people, and huge structures like the Great Pyramid were erected as a way to connect with the Law of One.

Closer toward their settlement, a huge feast was being prepared to mark this momentous occasion. Colorful tents had been set up, and musicians were brought in from neighboring communities. Another warm breeze skirted around the crowd and brought with it a cornucopia of rich scents to Lilith. The smells of spices, cooked meat, fresh bread, sweet dates, and juicy pomegranates made her stomach growl. A warm, rough hand tugged on her fingers.

"Relax, Lilith," Mica said, taking her hand in his. "And stop clasping your hands. There are no worries here."

"I am not worried," Lilith replied, caressing the outside of Mica's hand with her thumb. "It is the way I connect with myself."

He chuckled. "Perhaps one day we shall...connect?"

Lilith's eyes widened. Her heart pumped harder, stronger, faster. A trace of a smile lit up her face. "Perhaps."

"Put me down here!" She-Aba commanded, clicking her tongue and clapping her hands.

"As you wish, She-Aba," the four men said in unison.

Grunting, they lowered the elaborate chair to the sand. Two men offered their hands to help She-Aba off. She nodded curtly, took both hands, and gingerly stepped down. Her high heels sunk into the sand.

Tau laughed. "That is why I go barefoot, fire-head."

"Bare feet are not stylish, bug-boy!" She-Aba spat, trying to free herself from the sand.

"I see after one hundred years, nothing changes," a low voice announced.

"Anapa!" Tau shouted.

"Anapa?" She-Aba said, undoing her shoes.

143

Legend of the Timekeepers

Lilith turned to find the human-jackal hybrid standing behind her. He hadn't aged much. A smattering of white whiskers on his muzzle was the only tell-tale sign that he had grown any older. His dark eyes were still alert, still bright, and his rich, dark skin was smooth and sun-kissed. The only big change to his appearance was that he now wore a gold and lapis lazuli coif and a Babel necklace. Anapa's long pointed ears moved forward, causing the round, gold earring to jiggle.

"Hello, Tau," he replied, showing off his white canine teeth. "I am known as Anubis now,"

"That's impossible," Tau said, looking him over. "You look the same. How can it be that you've—"

"Barely aged?" Anapa said.

"I know!" She-Aba snapped her fingers. "You used some of my creams in the satchel I gave Rhea!"

Anapa frowned. "Hybrids do not need such things."

Lilith gasped. "The Book of Mysteries!"

"Yes," Anapa replied, adjusting the long gold and white schenti he wore around his hips. "Some of the potions scribed in it help to slow down age. Ajax-ol and Rhea chose to dilute their portions so they would not disrupt the balance of nature."

She-Aba patted her face. "Would you happen to know where the Book of Mysteries is kept?"

Tau snorted. "You'd need the full strength potion, fire-head!"

"I have missed you two," Anapa said, grinning as best he could.

"It seems you've repaid your debt to Etan," Lilith said, looking around at all the magnificent structures Ajax-ol had built over his lifetime.

"Not yet, but he's about to," an old man's voice cracked.

Ajax-ol and Rhea—now known as Duo-She-Dui and Mu-Elden—had joined them. Guards kept a tight circle around them as the crowd pushed in to get a closer look at the influential golden couple of the Black Land. A dark blue robe and a sash made of diamonds and pearls shrouded Ajax-ol's frail frame. His white hair still stuck out like a lion's mane in the breeze. Rhea wore her healer's robe and sash, and her shimmering hair was neatly combed back and held in place by a silver headband. Ajax-ol's glittering walking stick that She-Aba had crafted for him one hundred years ago now helped him negotiate the uneven desert sands.

Sharon Ledwith

Not far behind them, the white tusked beast loomed, swaying side to side. "I see Elie must have received the same potion too," Lilith said, pointing at her.

"No. The potion only works on humans or human-animal hybrids. That is Elie's granddaughter, Exina. She was born white, an auspicious sign, Rhea reminded us," Anapa said, then placed his hands together and bowed before Ajax-ol and Rhea. "It is good to see you again, my old friends."

"Who are you calling old?" Rhea said, smiling. She reached over to stroke his shiny black nose. "You look well, Anapa. Your new purpose suits you."

"What new purpose?" Tau asked. "Did you get a life seal reading?"

"Hybrids do not require such insights," Ajax-ol said, his voice sounding syrupy and sweet like drizzling honey. "He knew in his heart what was expected of him."

"So what did your heart tell you, Anapa?" Lilith asked.

Anapa nudged his canine muzzle toward the river where a large, red ferry boat was moored in front of the square stone building next to the river. A thin gauzy material acted as a canopy, and both the bow and stern were expertly carved into the shape of a sea shell.

"I don't get it," She-Aba said, squinting. "You still ferry people like you did in Atlantis. That's old news."

"Yes, but their destinations were all different places. Here, I chart a course for only one port," Anapa replied, moving both his pointy ears forward, "and provide safe passage to those who are ready to move on to their next life."

"Do you still weigh and measure all your passengers?" Tau asked.

Anapa nodded. "It is how I determine who is ready to take the journey, and who must be left behind."

"Well, let's hope we don't have to use your services anytime soon, Anapa," She-Aba said, winking. "I was just offered an apprenticeship with Iel, the head seamstress in the Temple Beautiful. I begin tomorrow."

"I have it on the highest authority that all of you won't be riding with me for a very long time, She-Aba," he replied, twitching his black nose. Then he dipped his human hand into a small pocket cut into the side of his schenti. "These are for Lilith and Mica."

145

Legend of the Timekeepers

"A Babel necklace?" Lilith said, releasing Mica's hand to accept his gift. "But...I speak the language of the Black Land fine, Anapa."

"That's debatable," Tau said, grinning.

"Why would we have need of these?" Mica asked, staring at the brilliant blue stone dangling from the orichalcum necklace.

"For your new purposes, my young friends," Ajax-ol said.

She-Aba jerked. She dropped her shoes. "What new purposes?"

"But, I don't understand, I just got assigned my new lifetime occupation," Lilith said. "We all have."

Rhea giggled. She sounded like a little girl on her first day of school. "You will have many occupations throughout your lifetime, Lilith. But you will have only one major purpose. This one will reflect what your soul knows and needs to accomplish." She bent to pick up She-Aba's shoes and handed them to her. "You just have to be ready to act on it. Do you see?"

Lilith stared at her Babel necklace. Belial's last words ripped through her mind like a cobra's fangs. *Time will flow through me, too.* She swallowed hard, knowing Belial would always be the darkest part of her, and of this world. Even Zurumu's curse had cut deep into their bloodline. Lilith sighed, lifted the Babel necklace over her head, and said, "I see now. We are to keep time safe by being Timekeepers. The Children of the Law of One have summoned all four of us to take on this important task. We must do as they bid."

"They did not summon me, Lilith," Mica said. He hung his head. "Istulo did."

Rhea cupped his chin with her palm and lifted his head. "Understand that you were tested, Mica. And you passed. All is as it should be. Now, you must follow your heart."

Lilith reached for Mica's Babel necklace, gently took it from him, and placed it around his neck. Then she took up his hand and said, "Listen to Rhea. After all, she is a seer."

"And remember, my young friends," Anapa said, touching his Babel. "This world is full of many languages, but there is only one true language—the language of *One*. Your Babels will aid to clear the garble so you can hear what is being said no matter what tongue is spoken to you."

The tinny sound of horns bugled through the air, accompanied by the low, rolling beats of drums. Lilith jumped and squeezed Mica's hand tighter.

146

"The time has come for the unveiling," Rhea announced. "Anapa, will you do the honor of revealing the Guardian of the Sands for us?"

Ajax-ol ambled over and clapped him on his dark, muscular shoulder. "Are you ready to wipe the slate and clear your debt, my dear, old friend?"

"This has been a long time coming," Anapa said, bowing. "I am ready."

Embellished chairs shrouded in shimmering silks and soft furs had been set up to face the covered massive monument. Lilith, Mica, Tau, and She-Aba took their places next to Ajax-ol and Rhea in the front row. High priests and priestesses sat behind them with the counselors, advisors, and dignitaries. Lilith spotted her father among them and waved. The craftspeople, sculptors, and architects stood in the back row, all dressed in their finest white linen schentis and sheaths. The air was getting hotter, yet it felt surprisingly light, charged with the anticipation of seeing Duo-She-Dui's newest creation, the Guardian of the Sands. Facing east, this monument would greet the new sun each day, bringing with it the promise of new things to come.

Suddenly, Rhea rose from her seat, opened her arms, and started to sing. Her voice, now older, was still as strong and as vibrant as ever. This was Anapa's sign to remove the veil. Pulling on a golden cord, Lilith heard him grunt a few times before the cover began to fall away and reveal what had taken years and years to sculpt. Lilith's eyes widened. The people, high priests and priestesses, counselors, merchants, traders, and artisans cheered and clapped.

"It's a lion!" a high priest remarked.

"It's a man!" a pregnant woman holding twin babies shouted.

"It's both!" a group of initiates hollered.

"Oh...my...Poseidon, it's Etan," Lilith said, staring at the stone likeness of him.

That knowing, secretive smile was immortalized for all the people to see. His fierce olive eyes. The red hue of his face. It was Etan, only he was portrayed with the full body of a lion to symbolize his courage and strength and wisdom. An enormous headdress had been fashioned to cover his mane. Bright yellow and black horizontal stripes decorated the headdress in a majestic way. Lilith began rubbing her hands back and forth, back and forth, then stopped, and brought them out and in, farther apart then closer

Legend of the Timekeepers

together. *This is time. It is nothing, yet it is everything,* she heard Etan whisper. Lilith shook her head, and smiled. *You knew, all along, didn't you, Etan? That all answers, everything we need to know, flows through us. And all we have to do is look, listen, and trust.* A gentle nudge roused Lilith from her thoughts.

"What do you think, Lilith?" Ajax-ol whispered.

"I...I think Etan's wisdom will live on forever." Then Lilith grinned, causing lines around the edge of her eyes to fan out. "Or at least keep people guessing for many years to come."

The End

Acknowledgements

I said it before and I'll say it again: Life is a team effort, and nothing is done without the help and support of others. The following people are in some way connected to the fabric of this work, to which I am eternally grateful:

Thank you to the staff at Mirror World Publishing; Justine Alley Dowsett, Murandy Damodred, and Robert Dowsett who gave this book a second chance. Hugs to my rock-star editor Tricia Schwaab who pushed my creative buttons so far I thought I was going through the change of life all over again. Seriously, Tricia, you made me a better writer. And finally, high fives to my book cover artist Kelly Shorten, who knew exactly what I wanted on her very first attempt at designing my beautiful cover—you are truly gifted.

A special shout out goes to my Wenches of Words family, especially to my cohort, Sloane Taylor. You Wenches have made this past year a special one with your show of kindness, support, caring, solidarity, and teamwork. Love you gals! May your lives be blessed with many bestsellers!

And last but not least, a big sloppy thank you to my hubby, Mike. You put up with enough of my melt-downs and tantrums to clear away any bad karma left between us. Again you acted as my pillar, my post, and more often than not, my anchor. God bless.

About the Author

Sharon Ledwith is the author of the middle-grade/young adult time travel series, THE LAST TIMEKEEPERS, and is represented by Walden House (Books & Stuff) for her teen psychic series, MYSTERIOUS TALES FROM FAIRY FALLS. When not writing, researching, or revising, she enjoys reading, exercising, anything arcane, and an occasional dram of scotch. Sharon lives a serene, yet busy life in a southern tourist region of Ontario, Canada, with her hubby, one spoiled yellow Labrador and a moody calico cat. Connect with her on her website: www.sharonledwith.com

Sharon Ledwith

To learn more about our authors and our current projects visit: www.mirrorworldpublishing.com, follow @MirrorWorldPub or like us at www.facebook.com/mirrorworldpublishing

We appreciate every like, tweet, facebook post and review and we love to hear from you. Please consider leaving us a review online or sending your thoughts and comments to info@mirrorworldpublishing.com

Thank you.

Legend of the Timekeepers

CPSIA information can be obtained
at www.ICGtesting.com
Printed in the USA
BVHW031820180321
602932BV00009B/120